Vienna Tales

Vienna
Tales

Stories selected
and translated by

Deborah Holmes

Edited by

Helen Constantine

OXFORD
UNIVERSITY PRESS

OXFORD
UNIVERSITY PRESS

Great Clarendon Street, Oxford, OX2 6DP,
United Kingdom

Oxford University Press is a department of the University of Oxford.
It furthers the University's objective of excellence in research, scholarship,
and education by publishing worldwide. Oxford is a registered trade mark of
Oxford University Press in the UK and in certain other countries

First Edition published in 2014

Impression: 1

Published in the United States of America by Oxford University Press
198 Madison Avenue, New York, NY 10016, United States of America

British Library Cataloguing in Publication Data

Data available

Library of Congress Control Number: 2014941325

ISBN 978-0-19-966979-0

Printed in Great Britain by
Clays Ltd, St Ives plc

Contents

Picture Credits

General Introduction to Vienna Tales

When I was a cook in Unterpurkersdorf *Altenheim*, a home for the aged in the suburbs of Vienna back in the 1960s—I think it was part of a Concordia work project of the kind students did in those days, before it was called the gap year and they all went round the world—I had to wear a spotless white apron and tie up my hair in an equally spotless white cap during the day. After work I took off my cap, let my hair down and twisted again to Chubby Checker and company. In the immediate surroundings of Unterpurkersdorf in the nearby *Naturpark*, there was some relaxation, apart from Chubby Checker, to be had, but on our days off we usually took the train from Unterpurkersdorf station into the centre to see the sights: the Stefansdom, the Prater, the Albertina museum, the Spanish Riding School, and then, further afield, the Palace of Schönbrunn.

Unterpurkersdorf was, and still is, a town outside Vienna in the Vienna Woods, and therefore my experience mirrors the structure of this volume: stories from the periphery of the capital, but looking inwards to its centre.

Several of the tales are set in the environs of, rather than in, the capital. In the 1840s the Prater amusement park, on an island outside the walls, was evoked fondly by Adalbert Stifter in his memoir; he calls it the 'garden of Vienna' and writes of meadows and copses and the rabbits on the path along the Danube where he can escape from the crowds in the city. At about the same time Heinrich Laube describes his arrival at an inn in Vienna with similar enthusiasm, and extols the 'city of paradise', full of cheerful, charming women and picturesque places, though he writes with tongue in cheek and a perceptive insight into the Viennese character. The photo opposite his story shows what Laube's point of arrival looks like in the twenty-first century, sadly now surrounded by office blocks, but also by housing developments which have improved the quality of life for many of the less well-off. Laube remarks: 'There is something touching about the fearful assiduousness with which the Viennese seek to uphold the belief that the good old days are still here in Vienna and that the city remains unchanged.' He himself suffered under the repressive regimes of his day and was imprisoned for his subversive activities.

By the turn of the nineteenth century Vienna was to some extent a police state, socially conservative, multicultural but antisemitic. But from 1867 to 1918, the end of the First World War, the Austro-Hungarian Empire did at least provide a vast zone in which a great variety of languages and cultures more or less vibrantly asserted their identities. The mid-nineteenth century was also the period of the feuilletonists, as described so vividly in a satirical portrait by Kürnberger included here. The feuilleton was a literary genre, originating from France and Germany, which might be compared to the review section of our modern newspapers, or even Facebook or Twitter, where cultural, not overtly political, subjects were discussed; much tittle-tattle was aired and there was often a great deal of gossip and back-biting.

Cities of course are constantly changing, and in the first years of the twentieth century Viennese life was by no means idyllic. However this was the period of creative activity that brought us, amongst others, Freud, Kokoschka, Klimt, Schiele, Schnitzler, and Schönberg. By the end of the First World War between 1918 and 1938, with much social division and outright conflict, life for many was very hard. In 1919 Anton Kuh writes in 'Lenin and Demel' of the effect of the class divisions in Vienna at that time. After the Anschluss in 1938 Hitler took control and Austria, already under an Austro-Fascist dictatorship, was assimilated into the Third Reich. 65,000 Jews were deported and murdered in concentration camps. As the war ended the Viennese suffered the Allied bombings and the city was occupied until 1955. Alexander Kluge's story, 'The Twilight of the Gods', documents the events that befell Wagner's opera, with the opera house itself being burnt down in a bombing raid. The subsequent discovery in the 1990s of the film of the performances is narrated here.

People, as well as places, can be peripheral. In Dinev's story about Spas in 2003, the refugee from Bulgaria is on the periphery of society. Readers will recognize the problems, so characteristic of our own time, encountered by many refugees arriving in a capital city and looking for work. In many of the collections of *City Tales* readers will find at least one story on this subject. In Vienna as in other cities at the beginning of the twenty-first century, Poles, Russians, Bosnians, Turks, Greeks, Romanians, and latterly Syrians, among others arriving in search of work, find themselves struggling to survive. Work for refugees is the Holy Grail, and *Arbeit* is the first word of German that Spas learns. But to work you need a work permit, and—to get a permit you need to be in work. Refugees can wait for years for a visa, living in squats, old train carriages, like Spas, or in other very poor accommodation.

Today, for those of us who choose to visit the city, but don't have to live on the edge of society, Vienna is considered to be one of the most 'liveable' cities in the world. We hope this literary journey, from the outside looking in, travelling through Vienna's woods and suburban streets into the heart of the city, will induce readers to make the acquaintance of writers who have lived and worked there, and thus gain an insight into what Vienna and the Viennese are 'really' like.

Introduction

Wien ist anders—Vienna is different. It's hard not to agree with the city's official slogan, omnipresent on billboards and in tourist brochures since the early 1990s. Vienna is different—different from the rest of Austria in its diversity and urban flair; different from other European capitals in its compact greenness and impeccable public transport system; different from what English-speaking visitors in particular seem to expect. Although the city's small, historic centre caters rather too exclusively to the luxury shopper, beyond this—and it can be walked through easily in twenty minutes or so—Vienna is a traveller's dream: as well as astonishingly reasonable food and accommodation, the city provides an impressive array of events open to whoever cares to attend, outdoor concerts, film showings, festivals, street parties, innumerable Christmas markets, food fairs. On the subject of which, the neat pun *Wien isst anders*—Vienna eats differently—has also become something of an official slogan, revealing both the childlike glee of the Viennese in word play and justified self-congratulation as regards the city's culinary traditions. Home of the Sachertorte and the schnitzel, to give but two notable examples, Vienna also offers fine wines, grown and served on sloping terraces within the city limits. The visitor sits, glass in hand, looking down over the 'Blue Danube', whose waters are not only famous in music and word, but also clean enough to provide miles of leafy beach in the long, hot summers. In many ways, it's immediately obvious why Vienna regularly tops the charts of cities with the highest quality of life worldwide.

When researching the stories for this collection, it therefore came as no surprise to discover that writers have often used Vienna as a byword for pleasure. In texts from the early to mid-nineteenth century in particular, the city stands for wine, women, and song, for a laid-back, playful—perhaps somewhat lax?—outlook on life that is invariably linked to its location as German culture's south-ernmost centre. The pieces I have included here by Heinrich Laube, Adalbert Stifter, and Ferdinand Kürnberger are very much in this vein. Kürnberger, a native of Vienna, plays up to the clichés of Viennese nonchalance and hedo-nism in a spirit of gentle self-irony. Laube and Stifter are two outsiders—Laube a Prussian, Stifter from the west of Austria—who knowingly allow Vienna to seduce them with its charms, and end up in an enjoyable if not uncritical daze.

Given the strength of this tradition, it comes as a surprise, as a shock even, to discover just how difficult it is to find more recent stories that take a light-hearted view of the city. The theme of the good life and of Vienna's beauty continues, but there are very few authors who do not dwell on elements of darkness or melancholy. Indeed, from the mid-twentieth century onwards, death itself seems to have become the preferred guide to the city in literature, as Austria's pre-eminent literary critic Wendelin Schmidt-Dengler once pointed out. Time and time again, narratives set in modern-day Vienna begin with the demise of a character or a funeral. Following the hints of an ever-constructive editor to balance the collection with some more cheerful pieces, many was the tale that I discarded—stories full of Viennese colour but characterized by negativity and loss: Heimito von Doderer's 'Tod einer Dame im Sommer' (Death of a Lady in Summer) for instance, and Thomas Bernhard's anguished 'Verbrechen eines Innsbrucker Kaufmannsohnes' (Crime of an Innsbruck Merchant's Son) or the blackly comical 'Ist es eine Komödie? Ist es eine Tragödie?' (Is it a Comedy? Is it a Tragedy?). Several such pieces remain: 'Six-nine-six-six-nine-nine' by Doron Rabinovici, a story about music, ghosts, and telephone sex, or else Eva Menasse's 'Envy', which shows that the twenty-first-century Viennese tale has by no means shaken off the shadow of death. Whether

Ingeborg Bachmann's 'O Happy Eyes' ends in an actual fatality or not is a moot point—something of a recurring feature in her short prose writings—and other stories in the collection are also pervaded by an atmosphere of finitude and endings: Christine Nöstlinger's 'Ottakringer-strasse' for example, or else Dimitré Dinev's 'Spas Sleeps'.

What are the reasons for this? Much has already been written about the cult of death in Vienna, of Viennese fascination with the 'schene Leich', which can mean either an exquisitely beautiful corpse or else a particularly sumptuous and well-organized funeral. In many ways, this seems to be the natural flip side to Viennese hedonism, as encapsulated countless times in popular *Wienerlieder* (Viennese songs): 'Es wird a Wein sein, und mir wer'n nimmer sein, d'rum g'niaß ma's Leb'n so lang's uns g'freut. / 'S wird schöne Maderln geb'n, und wir werd'n nimmer leb'n, D'rum greif ma zua, g'rad is's no Zeit' (there'll be wine galore, and we'll be no more, so enjoy yourself, don't stop and reason. / There'll be pretty girls to hold, and we'll have gone cold, so cling on to life's brief season). There is also a counter-reformatory, Baroque element that persists in Viennese culture, be it only as ironic quotation (Eva Menasse!), which favours the *memento mori*. But all of these reasons pale in comparison to Vienna's deadly twentieth-century history. Although it was one of the world's largest cities by 1900, it shrank rather than growing over the following hundred years. Decimated by starvation and epidemics after the First World War and by the Nazis' murderous racism 1938–45, Vienna's population has only recently begun to recover. Even now, it has still not regained the size of its *fin-de-siècle* glory days. The gaping holes left in the city's social and intellectual fabric by the expulsion or extermination of its Jewish population continue to preoccupy, if not torment, some of its finest writers. Vienna's historical losses are addressed repeatedly, either openly—as in Rabinovici's tale—or else as an ever-present, ominous substratum, as in Bachmann's story of Miranda, a woman who literally refuses to see Vienna for what it is.

To a certain extent, however, the sense of endings and limits in many of the tales is also simply a result of my initial idea for the collection. I wanted to concentrate on stories set at the city's margins. Perhaps more than any other modern European capital, Vienna is dominated by its natural surroundings—the Vienna Woods and the foothills of the Alps to the west, the arms of the Danube cutting through the city from north to south and the Pannonian plain stretching away to Hungary in the east. Modern developers have had relatively little opportunity to obscure this distinctive topography. The Iron Curtain descended less than forty miles away, and Vienna was left stranded in a backwater until the Cold War ended: roads and railways petered out towards this hermetic border. At least the regulation of the Danube was concluded during this period—no longer is the city plagued by catastrophes such as the flood that ends Franz Grillparzer's 'The Poor Fiddler', another tale regretfully excluded from this collection. Even now, as housing developments gradually begin to creep across the eastern plain and up into the Vienna Woods, clear differences remain between the appearance of the city's geographical 'regions'—and Vienna as a whole is still small enough for the visitor to explore each of these for him or herself.

There are also still many places where you can see into and out of the city with one exhilarating gaze. Laube's description of arriving in Vienna from the south first attracted me because of the familiar feeling it conveys of passing the Spinnerin am Kreuz and looking down over Vienna, despite almost two centuries' difference. And even from the centre, the vineyards of the Kahlenberg and Bisamberg remain visible, the two small mountains— confused by Miranda in Bachmann's story—that stand sentinel to the west and east of the Danube as it enters the city. This natural gateway directs wind and weather into Vienna, which is situated both literally and figuratively on a watershed between western and eastern Europe. Atlantic fronts clash with air from the steppes above the city, and centuries of cultural and political struggle have been conducted within it. Every metropolis is a melting pot, but Vienna's self-consciousness as either a 'gateway to the east' or else 'bulwark of the west' is especially acute. The threat of siege—real or imagined—recurs as a theme, taken up here by Anton Kuh in his account of deposed Habsburg aristocrats negotiating newly republican Vienna in 1919 (and what could be a more Viennese solution to their dilemmas than taking refuge in a coffeehouse?). However, whatever position writers take up in the interminable debate of East versus West, their descriptions of the city are informed by the same topography, the same climate and natural landmarks. A feeling of being, paradoxically, both at the centre of Europe and on its margins can be found again and again, mirrored in the microcosm of the city and its environs.

Partly as a way of evading, but partly also as a way of redefining these debates on the city's identity, authors of Vienna tales have often chosen to set their works at the city's edges, in the interstices between urban and rural life. They have also found transitional moods and moments in the city centre, which is dominated by its own series of 'natural' landmarks—labyrinthine parks and enormous green spaces, the Volksgarten, Stadtpark, Augarten and Prater, the banks of the Danube and the river Wien. Much of Vienna's built environment has remained unchanged for so long that it also seems natural—the craggy single peak of the Stefansdom, the crooked axis of Graben and Kärtnerstrasse and the bulk of the imperial Hofburg. What on earth, Kürnberger's blasé coffeehouse patron asks, is an author to write about in Vienna, where everything always stays the same? From the early 1860s onwards, shortly after this text by Kürnberger was first published, the inner city wall was gradually demolished and the transportation network modernized. Even then, however, the city fathers chose conservative solutions: the famous Ringstrasse that replaced Vienna's bastions still traces the same semi-circle, dividing the centre from the outlying districts. The first urban railway lines were opened late for a metropolis the size of Vienna—1898—and constructed around the city's existing features rather than ploughing through or under them. Vienna's constancy and harmony with its natural surroundings has been idealized by generations of writers seeking to capture the secret of its charm. At the same time, as my collection goes some way to showing, a counter-tradition has grown up of consciously seeking the seamy, the corrupt, and the horrific beneath the city's attractive exterior. Here the idyllic images of woods and water, mountains and parks appear in ironic subversions, used to throw the darker episodes of Vienna's history into starker relief.

In keeping with the original theme of the collection, the stories are arranged geographically rather than chronologically, around and through the city from west to east and back again. I begin and end with two pieces by Arthur Schnitzler (1862–1931), a writer who lived and worked in Vienna throughout his life, and whose oeuvre is remarkable for its precise and yet poetic evocations of the city. No matter how impressionistic, his descriptions of Vienna's centre can always be followed step by step with a map in hand: street names, addresses, cafés and amenities of the time are all there. Away from the centre, the topography in his works becomes less determinate, but the sense of place, paradoxically, seems even stronger. The two stories selected here 'The Four-poster Bed' and 'Out for a Walk' are prime examples of this, introducing us to the Vororte west of the city that used to be a half-rural, half-urban no-man's land between Vienna's suburbs and the outlying villages and is now subsumed in the fifteenth to nineteenth districts. This is a setting to which Schnitzler returns, for the location of the masked ball gate-crashed by Fridolin in the extraordinary 'Dream Story' of 1926. 'The Four-poster Bed' and 'Out for a Walk' are early works, written sometime between 1891 and 1893. Neither story was anthologized during Schnitzler's lifetime, nor did they make it into the collected works that Schnitzler selected for publication by Fischer in 1922. They are effectively rejects and have never been translated before, not even appearing in book form until 1977 (in the posthumous *Gesammelte*

Werke also published by Fischer). However, they not only fit in perfectly with my theme of the city's margins, but are also perfectly rounded stories, which makes their marginal status in Schnitzler's oeuvre even more intriguing. They illustrate in miniature a much discussed characteristic of all his writing: its repetitive nature and obsessive variation of a limited number of themes—love, death, Vienna. Schnitzler is a gift to every anthology, because it is arguably easier to do him justice with one or two short pieces than other Viennese writers from the same period with more varied themes such as, for example, Musil or Hofmannsthal.

No-one actually dies in either 'Out for a Walk' or 'The Four-poster Bed', but lots of things come to an end—and at the beginning of both texts, we find ourselves physically at the very edge of the city, beyond the outer *Linie* or *Linienwall*. The composition of the two stories was swiftly followed by another ending, the demolition in 1894 of this last line of Vienna's historic fortifications, making way for a wave of building expansion that swept away the Vororte as Schnitzler describes them here. Both stories share almost identical openings, but develop very differently. 'The Four-poster Bed' is a bittersweet love story between a young gentleman from the city centre and a 'süßes Mädel' ('sweet maid') from the Vorstadt— one of the many lissom, sexually available lower-middle-class females so central as a concept in Schnitzler's works and yet often so peripheral as characters. 'Out for a Walk' by contrast evokes the mood of city's periphery as the setting for a heated debate between four young men— part flippant, part desperate—as to what Vienna might 'mean' and whether or not it has a soul. They are however in total agreement as regards its fickleness and the pitfalls of seeking success and recognition there. 'Out for a Walk' enriches my anthology not only with references to Viennese topography, but also to its literary history. The four friends would have been immediately recognizable to readers of the time as portraits of the central clique of 'Young Vienna': Schnitzler, Hofmannsthal, Felix Salten, and Richard Beer-Hofmann. The problem they discuss of how to reconcile the (self-)critical and experimental with local patriotism and tradition was one of the chief dilemmas of Viennese Modernism.

From the western outskirts of the city, the collection takes us on excursions up into the Vienna Woods with Joseph Roth and Friedericke Mayröcker. Mayröcker also plumbs the city's depths, represented here by its Second World War bomb shelters. The descent into Vienna's underworld continues with Alexander Kluge's documentary-style description of how Wagner was recorded in cellars around the State Opera during Allied raids in spring 1945. We surface again in the city centre to take a satirical look at the effects of the First World War with

Anton Kuh's account of Konditorei Demel, a coffeehouse and cake shop patronized by the Habsburgs themselves, whose sumptuous window displays and uniformed waitresses continue to grace the Kohlmarkt today. Many of the photographs featured here were selected over lunch in Demel's 'smoking salon', sunk deep in armchairs that would surely still be feudal enough to put the barons and counts in Kuh's piece at their ease. Some writers consider the carefully cultivated sense of historical continuity in Vienna's city centre disturbing—*unheimlich*, to use a term favoured by one of its most famous former inhabitants, Sigmund Freud. Bachmann's Miranda in 'O Happy Eyes' is at once deeply attached to her home in the central Blutgasse and at the same time determined to distance herself from the realities of life in the city. By the story's end she seems to have achieved her ambition, if not by the means originally intended.

To escape the burden of history, we then take a fresh run-up at the city, entering it from the south with Laube in the mid-1830s. Twenty years later, Kürnberger's amusing anatomy of Vienna's various 'species' of journalist suggests several different approaches or perspectives. His final example, that of the 'social feuilletonist' or *Feuilletonistus aequivocus*, gives us a brief glimpse of what were then Vienna's newly forming industrial suburbs, another vantage point from which to see the city from its margins. The next piece, by the Bulgarian-born Dimitré Dinev, is one of many examples of how Vienna's literary scene has been revitalized by immigrant writers in recent years. Its unassuming hero Spas is an asylum seeker whose view of the city throws a whole new light on the traditional connotations of its topography.

We first and last see Spas in the third district, Wien Landstraße, to the south-east of the centre—said to have been considered by Metternich as the beginning of the Balkans. The second short piece I have selected by Joseph Roth, 'The Spring Ship', encapsulates beautifully the feeling of wanderlust this part of the city inspires with its open skies and the Danube canal leading further south to far-away places... The canal also marks the dividing line between the third and second district, the latter dominated by the Prater, Vienna's 'green lung'—an immense, teardrop-shaped park that combines fairground, football stadium, conference centres, pubs, clubs, meadows, swamps, and primordial woodland. The proportions of this mixture may have changed over the years, but as the stories here by Stifter and Canetti show, its unique attraction has remained constant. Although it is such a varied and open space, the Prater represents a concentration of conflicting traditions typical of Vienna as a whole. Originally a Habsburg hunting ground and the exclusive preserve of a dynastic elite, it was opened to the public in 1766 under Emperor Josef II, a great

Enlightenment reformer. The upper classes continued to use the Prater for riding, racing, and hunting into the 1920s, but at the same time it became a much-loved site of popular entertainment and of popular protest. From 1890 right up to the present, streams of workers have marked Labour Day in Vienna with marches through the Prater. And Vienna's Communist movement, although otherwise moribund, still manages to host the enormously successful Volksstimmefest ('people's voice' party) there every year. Veza Canetti's story refers to these traditions in the political bent of her unabashed young protagonist. Canetti herself was closely associated with 'Red Vienna', the Social Democrat administration that attempted to revolutionize the city after the First World War, before a proto-fascist putsch put an end to it and to any realistic chance of being able to hold out against Hitler.

Childhood experience of the city is central not only to Canetti's tale, but also to Christine Nöstlinger's description of the Ottakringerstrasse, the busy street that divides the sixteenth from the seventeenth district. In both pieces, any sentimentality is counterbalanced by an ironic, at times surreal edge—as one would expect from these socially critical, unconventional authors. Nöstlinger takes us close to the city's western edge, where the villa of the charismatic but ultimately isolated literature professor in Menasse's 'Envy' is to be found. Sergio, the composer in Rabinovici's tale, also takes refuge in a suburb, although it is not made clear which: musicians have found inspiration throughout the city and its history, as numerous plaques on walls show. Equally, the events leading up to the Holocaust, fundamental to Rabinovici's mysterious narrative, could also have taken place in any district of Vienna. In 'Merry-go-round', Joseph Roth takes us back out to the Vororte, where Schnitzler's four friends are 'Out for a Walk', concluding the anthology. The combination of little-known pieces by writers already indelibly associated with Vienna and tales by contemporary authors translated here for the first time will, I hope, give the reader a new perspective on the city, seen from its literary margins.

The Four-poster Bed

Arthur Schnitzler

Embers of June sun burnt down slowly. We had left the city, and were far beyond the outer wall; a long row of tall, identical houses stretched away from us, glistening an ugly, yellow colour. Men in shirtsleeves stood at the many open windows, following the clamorous tram with vacant eyes. Blowsy women in loose chemises stared into the distance. Grimy children played noisily in the streets, and on the dull green meadows that began here and turned into gentle hill country further out, we saw common folk who yearned for fresher air without knowing it: little boys and girls, rolling on the ground or running to and fro, soldiers smoking cheap cigars with idiotically cheerful off-duty faces, streetwalkers in twos and threes laughing loudly as they strode over the fields, and the occasional solitary wanderer who had ventured out to savour the atmosphere of this peculiar no-man's land where the city gradually comes to an end, its raw, fearful panting ceasing in a weary, thankful sigh.

That was how the two of us, Hans and I, came to be out there today, giving in once again to the yearning that sometimes possessed us, a yearning to see something end, to pursue dying sounds and fading colours, to witness gradual transitions. Hints of this profound and melancholy charm were always to be found there, and we had taken to strolling around the area already years before. Although barely in better spirits than today, we had greater inner wealth at our disposal then: it was a time when we still transfigured the poverty of existence with the immense compassion of youth and individuals rose up before us out of the crowd that has now become a brutal, hostile mass in our eyes.

The last embers of sunset died down. Cool shadows crept up the houses, slowly, until they disappeared on the roofs. All that remained, way out on the last buildings, was a reddish, aching glow.

Now we had reached the final houses. The road came to an abrupt stop; this was where the city ended. We turned and looked back at the cloud of dust and vapour—out of which the streets seemed to crawl towards us with an enormous effort—and stood still, waiting to be enveloped by the voluptuous folds of longed-for twilight.

'Isn't it as though there are places where the city forgets to grow?' Hans remarked. 'There are points where its boundaries seem to advance on the hills from one day to the next, as though it were rushing forward, but here it seems to stand still. I've hardly noticed any changes since I moved away from here, and that must be twenty years ago now. There are some ghastly apartment blocks over there by the house that used to be the very last one—yes, the very last— but they don't signify, in my eyes, they simply don't exist.'

He looked back at the small, single-storey grey house, his eyes dwelling on it almost with affection. After a little while however his features changed, and his expression became one of melancholy distaste.

'Even that came to such a stupid end,' he said then, in a low voice.

I knew what he was thinking of. He had lived in that house with a sweet, darling girl for many months and like so many love stories, it had come to a gradual, almost imperceptible end, without any aftershocks.

'What on earth', I asked him, 'makes you say "stupid end"? The end always seems stupid just because it is the end, and all that is left of the spring-like radiance of the beginning is a weak, pathetic glimmer that gradually sets over our feelings. The end is stupid in any case, whether it is sudden unfaithfulness or a dreadful argument or a petering out, an evaporating into nothingness like your affair with Anna back then. I am right, aren't I? You just grew tired of each other with time?'

He looked at me with a smile. 'So you want the story to have a moral, do you? Well, the way things ended between Anna and myself is very moral in the final instance. It's a cautionary tale that could even be told to children if it didn't begin with passionate desire and if eternal justice had not used such indecorous means to teach a lesson about wisdom and life.'

'So I don't know the whole of that old story after all?'

'Of course you do, more or less. But you see, when those final rays played on the windows just now, I remembered the last hour of our love more clearly than ever before. It was a melancholy summer evening just like today, and just like today, the hazy, trembling rays were fading behind the hills over there.'

'Well?' I probed.

He told the tale in a low voice: 'We really did love each other, as you know. After the first few weeks when spring storms raged over and above us, it turned into a kind of married life that we couldn't imagine ever coming to an end. The little room we lived in together was bright and snug. All at once, I've no idea why or how, we were seized

by a curious yearning. We were still content with everything, though. We cared nothing for the size of the room,
the rickety table, the two ugly chairs and the hanging clock
that refused to work. But one night, when we felt as though
we must be in a fairytale—like bewitched royalty—the
lowly bed was suddenly no longer good enough for us.
I don't know why. Our love was immense and fantastical;
in our minds she wore pearls around her neck and dia-
monds and emeralds in her hair and I sported the crimson
cloak of a young prince: it was just pathetic that we should
have to spend our blissful nights between roughly woven
linen and scratchy blankets on a narrow, squeaky bed-
stead. Then and there, we decided to change our setting.
We would embark on a life of hard work, we would save,
both of us, in order to surround ourselves with all the
insignia of our fairytale splendour. This was how it should
be: heavy velvet curtains draped from yonder lintel, outlandish, obscure pictures on the walls, shimmering green
silk shrouding the windows and a soft red cloth on the
table, flowers in that corner and this, and a lamp with
dreamy shades hanging from the ceiling, its light both
melancholy and sweet. In the midst of all this finery, we
would lie on a yielding, tender, resting place with slender
wooden columns bearing darkly glowing, noble silk that
obeyed the slightest touch on a brightly-coloured cord. We
were to bury ourselves in this bed, the muted light of the

lamp only penetrating the trembling silk with difficulty, as though from a great distance. I don't know if she imagined it in exactly the same way, but it was to be beautiful, that much was certain, and as we were young and very much in love, what we yearned for most and thought about most often was the four-poster bed.

'After a little while, we actually managed to save enough money—of course, we couldn't afford as splendid a bed as we dreamed of, but we had to have one and soon, soon, that was for sure. We spoke about it every night. We were living in a period of transition, we had to get through it as quickly as possible. A nervous, tearful impatience plagued us, and when I think back to that time, it seems to me that we hardly made love any more; if only this time of waiting were over—that was our one thought. Ah, finally, finally—the last night! I remember it well. We cried. I think we were more chaste than ever before. She fell asleep in my arms, teardrops still clinging to her cheeks. I saw their gleam in the flicker of the candle that burnt beside us. We were expecting the bed to arrive the following morning. When it was time to get up, we held one another tightly. I remember very clearly that, with a stab of pain, the words suddenly shot through my head: it's all over now! I didn't think any more of it, they were just words. In the afternoon we met on the street. I hadn't been home during the day; she told me that 'it' had already arrived. I didn't dare ask her what it was like, what it looked like in our room. We decided to go for a walk, we didn't have the courage to return home yet. Filled with foreboding, and so sad, so heart-wrenchingly sad, we wandered over the fields. Just look out there, I feel as though I can see the two of us as we were twenty years ago, pacing the wasteland so slowly and painfully. We hardly said a word. The afternoon was oppressive and sombre. Not even the approaching evening promised respite. We did not walk arm-in-arm as usual. We didn't feel we should. Finally—it must have been about the same time as it is now—we headed in the direction that would take us home and when we reached the front door, we smiled at one another. But what a smile! So mute, so weary, so diffident. And then upstairs and then our room. There it was against the wall, opposite the window and there they were, the rays that you can see playing on the windows over there, flickering and trembling on the floor. They crept up onto the four-poster bed and lay on its silken folds, exhausted and dying. How pathetic, how heartbreaking it all was.

'We stood in front of the bed for a long time, we waited until the sun had gone down. And Anna nestled against me and in her fixed expression I could see how deadly shocked she was that she no longer felt anything, absolutely nothing at all. And when I took her head in my hands, these hands of mine no longer had the feeling of holding a sweet, beloved little head, no, not at all, not at all.

'We could have carried on loving one another in perfect accord for a little while longer. Quite contentedly, and it would have been a gradual, merciful death, without unpleasant surprises, without desperate fights. We refused this act of grace! We wanted to force back the fleeting bliss that was trying to slip away quietly without us noticing. How stupid we were! It all became clear to me on that summer evening, and it was as well for me that I knew. It had come upon Anna like the sudden realization of approaching death, and she wasn't able to truly comprehend what was happening.

'It grew late, night fell... the night with its lies and beauty. We buried ourselves, prince and princess, in our fairytale bower and laughed, but our laughter did not ring true—we rejoiced, but with tears in our eyes.

'Morning came, ah, the morning. She was still asleep, a quiet smile around her mouth... of course, for now she was dreaming... and I left. How beautiful it would have been, how gloriously liberated I would have felt if I had never returned! If only we had both had the courage, right then, the first night in our four-poster bed. But now I knew how it had to happen. That night had given me a foretaste of what would follow: desire without joy, the mad, vain attempt to recapture happiness, the agonized longing for heedless bliss—the best that we can experience—and the deepest misfortune of knowing that we are lying, of knowing that we are being lied to! Yes, that had to come, and it did—the many summer nights when our love died! And we saw and knew, but we carried on joking and neither of us said anything to the other. And then we tormented each other, because we had to lie, and then we stopped trusting one another, because we no longer trusted ourselves. And instead of peacefully passing away, as love should, there were dreadful dying agonies with a thousand exquisite tortures, and we parted with poisoned memories . . . '

Now he fell silent, and twilight had fallen. We had walked out further into the meadow as we talked and I could no longer see the window behind which Hans had lived out his moral tale. It lay in darkness like all the others. And I wondered how often since then the same story as the secret adventure of my dear Hans had played out behind that windowpane and all the others, and how rarely those involved would have realized what was happening. Our own experience is the deepest of secrets. The good among us agonize over it in all honesty, but still would not want to exchange this honourable, sacred pain for that which spares the others our suffering: blithe ignorance and an utter refusal to see.

Day Out*

Joseph Roth

You can smell the new wine already at Schottentor, the number 38 tram is tipsy and staggers off hung with bunches of human bodies. In the bright sunlight, noses pearl with sweaty dew. The driver, wedged in, puffs and blows like a machine, 76 HP. Rucksacks, still slack but swelling slightly in expectation of spoils from the country. Hobnailed mountain boots, re-soled seven times over, tread on the corns of fellow passengers. Human flesh steams on the rear platform, accelerating the tempo of the wheels.

Past garden fences hung with green swags that almost brush the tram window. Dogs howl in a backyard. The

* 'Ausflug', published under the pseudonym 'Josephus' in *Der Neue Tag*, 28 March 1920.

speeding tram enrages a poodle, locked in somewhere. It thinks the noisy red and yellow monster is making fun of it. Young bean plants send out slender, premature tendrils, tentatively exploring. Coquettish bow windows are half veiled with wild vines, afraid of getting freckles. A garden gate gets a make-over in white. Fumes rise from the oil paint in the warm sunshine.

End of the line. Green public conveniences with elevated prices, ticket collector with sheets of newspaper, clipping world history, on wooden seats rubbed smooth by trouser bottoms. The open tram spits people. First breath of nature heartens courting couples. Somewhere a kiss falls like a solitary raindrop in the silence.

'Café-Restaurant'. Headwaiter, spotless shirtfront, gleaming parting, each strand carefully counted, pomade right and left, oily as whipped cream. Noiseless gestures. Fingers move on rubber soles. His apprentice, toddler in a tailcoat, has shiny, red-brown cheeks with light peachy down. He smells of milk, like a sucking babe.

One of the corner windows has been occupied by a pack of black marketeers. Overcoats and jackets with belts in which, strangely, there are no hand grenades. Broad fingernails polished this very morning by the hairdresser gleam like shards of glass. Table manners just bought, still stiff and new; you can see the price tag dangling on them.

Six, seven of them. Their shiny green ties are very loud.
They order 'choc'lit'. Seven cups of hot choc'lit.

'Anything else?' murmurs the waiter with a bow.

'Seven Sachertorte!' says one. He pays. Hard currency
at his command, hand in trouser pocket, fingers squirming
like captive rabbits. The bowed legs of a removal man.
Eyes without lashes, brows barely there, as if drawn with a
hesitant line of kohl.

'Seven Sachertorte!' The waiter smiles, oily-smooth
superiority. 'Johnny, bring these gentlemen some *cake*!'

The gentlemen are speechless. Didn't they just order
Sachertorte? Their behaviour is muted. Even their ties
have suddenly fallen silent. The one with his hands in his
pockets considers: is cake Sachertorte?

Johnny brings cake. Seventy fingers crumble it. Dunk
cake into choc'lit like sponges into water. Gurgling slurps
to end with. It sounds like bursts of water down a broken
drain.

Singing on the road back into town. 'The little birds in
the greenwood'. Innocuousness created by dint of violent
effort. Picture-book tourists' outfits. Women's faces wiped
clean of powder by the wind. City dwellers in the 'open
countryside'.

On the spring meadow, twenty-five paper bags fly up
suddenly. A cigarette glows red in the gathering twilight.
Returning passengers sway towards the tram stop as

top-heavy as loaded hay wagons heading for the barn, Tyrolean hats pushed back on their heads, enjoying themselves at all costs.

There's a rush for the tram. Can't-keep-us-down dialect predominates.[*] Heartburn sufferers swallow the new wine once more.

The first streets are silent, ducking in fear of the homecomers. The electric tram flashes through a quiet street like a wild panic. And over liverish, yellow gaslights, a crescent moon laughs sardonically to itself.

---

[*] A reference to the popular saying 'Der echte Wiener geht nicht unter'—you can't keep a true Viennese down or the true Viennese never gives up.

Vienna 1924 to . . .

Friedericke Mayröcker

. . . the old man and child. Gone held holding hands they plod apart . . . unreceding on . . . that shade a woman's. An old woman's.

and walked so long in this city the child and walked holding the hand of her father the child and walked holding the hand of her mother so long, and stood in front of the rotating *automatic buffet* in the Mariahilferstrasse, asked for an open sandwich with egg. Yes, that one! the child calls out, taps with the tip of her finger against the glass. That's too expensive, says father, have a different one. He puts the coin in, bread roll with processed meat uncurls toward the child, child wolfs down roll. They pass the Ruprechtskirche, father says: the oldest church in Vienna, father says, child barely listens, already listened so often when father talks. The child is probably thinking of other things, father says: we're going in—throw that roll away! Child cries, throws roll in the gutter, follows with bowed head, feels hurt.

> *...Back unsay shades can go. Go and come again. No. Shades cannot go. Much less come again. Nor bowed old woman's back. Nor old man and child. Nor foreskull and stare. Blur yes. Shades can blur....*

We're going on a trip to Kahlenberg, says father, child and mother are pleased, we'll take sandwiches with us so that we don't need to go anywhere to eat, says father, we've enough money for the tram, says father. We'll walk over to Leopoldsberg, says mother, and over the ridge back to Nussdorf.[*]

> *...Said is missaid. Whenever said said said missaid...Back is on. Somehow on...Say better worse now all gone save trunks from now....Topless baseless hindtrunks. Legless plodding on. Left right unreceding on.*

Father takes snapshots, Box Tengor, nice little pictures with zig-zag edges, mother unpacks the provisions, white cloth napkin on her knees. Buttered bread from metal tin,

---

[*] Mountainous locations in the Vienna Woods on the western edge of the city.

laid together in the middle, a hardboiled egg, a minute saltcellar. The child climbs a cliff spur, looks out into the landscape, down under down over to the Danube. Mother offers lemon tea from a thermos flask with a felt cover, the child doesn't want to eat doesn't want to drink, stays put on her look-out post, soaks up the view at her feet, landscape not quite spring marchcold breeze, ponytail flies. Mother calls: come and eat or there'll be nothing left.

Air raid alarm, the child hurries with the mother into the shelter, a little case with documents and valuables under her arm. Wiedner Hauptstrasse 96, the sirens howl, they hunker down in the candlelight, the earth shakes, prayers and cries of fear, old men and women, dogs whining.

The child reads in Wotruba's memoirs, Wotruba writes: when I'm dead, I'll be as big as the Stefansdom. The child thinks about this, talks about it with a schoolfriend, private primary school Nikolsdorfergasse 8, 5th district.

The spiritus flower, says mother, your great aunts have started using oil lamps to save money, says mother. When we visit them, they give us a jar of apricot jam as a present.

The child watches as the Florianikirche in the middle of the Wiedner Hauptstrasse is demolished, the child is upset. The child receives holy baptism first holy communion holy confirmation. It wears a light grey crêpe dress made by mother, white ankle socks and black patent leather shoes, the confirmation float is already waiting, decorated with white artificial flowers. It is a warm, rainy day in May. Let's go to the Prater, says the child's god-mother, the child doesn't know what to say. All those candles, she thinks, the balloons. On the photographs her smile looks strained. She doesn't feel at ease, anywhere. Mother protects her, takes her side, encourages the child. They take the train to Baden together, go for walks in Helenental, surrounded by mighty ferns, humming and buzzing in the fern forest, it's such a hot day. They rarely speak, hold hands when it gets steep. The child's cape, the mother's sun hat . . . the whirl of the city. The bushel light, says mother, you shouldn't hide your light under a bushel.

Heaven and hell, the adult child says, balancing act life and Vienna.

. . . In the skull all gone. . . . Long sudden gone . . . Somehow on. Anyhow on . . .

(Quotations (italic): Samuel Beckett, *Worstward Ho*)

The Twilight of the Gods in Vienna

Alexander Kluge

(for Heiner Müller)

The way the twentieth century lays hold of music.

Gerard Schlesinger, Cahiers du Cinéma

Whatever is not broken cannot be saved.

H. Müller, Cruel Beauty of an Opera Recording

In March 1945 the metropolis of Vienna was surrounded by Soviet assault detachments. The only remaining connection to the Reich by land was to the north and north-west. This was the moment at which the *Gauleiter* and

Reichsverteidigungskommissar Baldur von Schirach, ruler of the city, commanded a final gala performance of 'Twilight of the Gods'. In the hopeless situation in which the city and the Reich found themselves, the plan was to broadcast the despair of the Nibelungs as set to music by Richard Wagner (but also the hope of resurgence contained in the final chords) on all the radio channels in southeast Europe that were still in German hands. 'The Reich may fall, but this music must remain ours.' The doors of the opera house were reopened, having been locked since the discontinuation of performances in October. Members of the orchestra were transported back from the fronts to the *Gauhauptstadt* Vienna. The night before one of the dress rehearsals (with orchestra and costumes, but without the conflagration of Valhalla in the third act—the final rehearsal was to be recorded and broadcast on radio, it was decided to dispense with an actual premiere), US squadrons flew from Italy to Vienna and bombarded the city centre. FIRE GUTTED THE OPERA.

Subsequently, the orchestra rehearsed in groups, divided up between various underground air raid shelters across the city. The left side of the orchestra worked in five groups in the cellars of buildings on the Ring; the right side of the orchestra—including the timpani—in four cellars on Kärtner Strasse and its side streets. The singers were divided up between the orchestra groups. They were instructed to perform 'like instruments'. They could not of course relate to one another as they were singing in different cellars. The musical director sat in the wine cellar of a public house, devoid at first of any connection, but soon in touch with all of the cellars by means of FIELD TELEPHONES.

Impact of artillery shells round about. During the rehearsals, two day-long attacks were mounted on the city by the US air force. Heavy artillery defence units based in nearby bunkers kept up fire on long-range Soviet batteries. Members of the infantry and railwaymen were assigned to the groups of rehearsing musicians as messengers. The information passed on in this way was supplemented by the field telephones, which did not just link the conductor with the various sections of the orchestra but also the orchestra groups to one another. The sounds produced by the nearby rehearsal groups and transmitted via these telephone lines were amplified in each case by loudspeakers. In this way, the musicians were able to gain a rough idea of what the other, separate ensembles were playing, while they themselves played the parts of the score for which they were responsible. Later, the musical director took to hurrying from cellar to cellar to give instructions in person. ATTENTION HAS TO BE PAID, HE SAID, TO COMPLETELY DIFFERENT THINGS THAN AT A DRESS REHEARSAL WHERE ALL ARE PRESENT.

The sound was also completely different. The noises of the final battle over Vienna could not be filtered out and the orchestral fragments produced did not result in a unified acoustic outcome. As Vienna's bridges were under threat, the commanding General Rendulic passed on a warning to the staff of the *Reichsverteidigungskommissar*. If the singers and orchestra were to be saved, they must be removed from the city to the west of Austria immediately. Instead of waiting for the final dress rehearsal, improvisation was called for. Upon hearing this, the *Reichsverteidigungskommissar*, still a young man, gave the order that the music as rehearsed thus far was to be recorded for broadcast straight away, that very day. In accordance with his command, recording of the 'fragments' of 'Twilight of the Gods' was begun at 11.30 with the first scene of the third act (Siegfried and the Rhine Maidens).

Playing continued until the end of the third scene of the third act. The first and second acts of the music drama were to follow. The intention was to piece the recordings together in the broadcasting studio or else, after the original master tapes had been flown out of Vienna, to reconstitute the work and broadcast it as a whole from the radio station in Salzburg, which was still in the hands of the Reich.

However, BY CHANCE three thousand metres of 35mm Agfa colour film were still in storage in the city of Vienna. Lieutenant Colonel Gerd Jänicke (General Staff) had four propaganda companies under his command, which he had concentrated in the besieged area in and around Vienna, determined to carry out his intention to film the city's downfall. Now he put his resolution into action. He ordered that the orchestra's efforts be captured in images and sound, although nothing could be done about the noise of the camera as no blimp* was available. To Jänicke, filming the final act of 'Twilight of the Gods' seemed the crowning glory of seven years of dedicated activity as chronicler and propagandist. There was nothing to hide; instead, staying power was to be documented, showing what would remain of the German Reich when all else perished: German music.

The third act and parts of the first act were filmed with five cameras and all the necessary sound recording equipment. Flak searchlights were set up to illuminate the scene: they shone on the cellar walls and gave a lurid indirect light. Considerable improvisation was called for to create an impression of wholeness: for example, singers and parts of the orchestra in cellars not documented by the film

* A protective casing that absorbs noise, muffling the sounds made by the camera itself [author's original footnote].

groups were included in the performance via two-way radio and recorded on 17.5mm perforated magnetic film; they were mixed in later on. Although an attempt was made to produce a finished, overall sound for the third act/first scene, by the second and third scenes of the third act, listeners were to be presented with a series of fragments. These scenes were heard and seen in the recording nine times, one after the other: a different cacophonous part of the score each time, as rehearsed in each separate cellar.

The civilian management of Radio Salzburg displayed the institutional cowardice typical of broadcasting corporations. Receipt of the recording of 'Twilight of the Gods', made up of many different unequal parts, was confirmed, but it was judged unfit to be broadcast for 'reasons of quality'. Telephone calls from the staff of the *Reichsverteidigungskommissar* failed to overturn this judgement. As if peacetime standards of quality were relevant at this juncture in the fortunes of the Reich! said the officer responsible for the operation in Schirach's staff, Captain von Tuscheck. But the civilian broadcasting directors in Salzburg remained unmoved. They broadcast one reel of the third act of 'Twilight of the Gods' and then nothing but march music until Salzburg was handed over to the victors.

In the meantime, the propaganda troops of Lieutenant Colonel Jänicke made sure that their undeveloped negatives and sound recordings were safely stored in a garage in the Vienna Hofburg. The intention was to have them sent to Oslo or Narvik in one of the last aircraft to leave Vienna. There was a film laboratory in the north. The recordings were to be kept from falling into the hands of the enemy; they represented a final missive from the embattled Reich. In contrast to 1918, bodies, tanks, and cities were blown to pieces at the end of the war, but minds and spirit remained intact. Theoretically, said Jänicke, even if all other means of defence are destroyed, ultimate victory is still possible through will-power and the weapons of the spirit. This holds true for the weapon of music above all.

It was no longer possible to fly the recording of 'The Twilight of the Gods' out of Vienna as there were no more vehicles available to transport the film canisters to the airport.

In the meantime, night had fallen. The musicians emerged from their cellars into the open. Infantry sergeants led them through the city centre under random fire. They were loaded onto buses and driven out of Vienna (the last to leave the trap as it closed). They greeted the morrow in rural surroundings. Billeted on farms in the Linz area, they found themselves arrested by American troops only a few days later.

The film canisters in the garage, still correctly labelled, were seized by Soviet officers and duly forgotten. A Georgian colonel who spoke French gave the lot to a Tartar lieutenant colonel, who could read German (a fact he only revealed to friends he could trust, needless to say, and not to his colleague from Georgia). The lieutenant colonel had the undeveloped films taken back to his garrison town of Sotschi, where they lay untouched for decades in the cellar of the municipal museum.

In 1991, after the breakup of the Soviet empire, this holding was discovered by a young composer who described himself as Luigi Nono's agent in Russia. He had followed a lead in a specialist Crimean music journal, which can be called up on the *internet* as a single page. Without ever having seen any of the material himself or knowing the place where it was stored, the young man organized its transport to a film studio in Hungary, where he had the films developed. The positives were sent to Venice. His intention was to play the sound track in the tenth year after Luigi Nono's death in the cathedral in Venice.

A cutter assistant of Jean-Luc Godard who had heard about this transfer, insisted nevertheless that the materials be re-sequenced in Paris in the film labs of the Cinétype Studios, and played the three thousand metres of film with sound and images to a group of people who worked for the *Cahiers du Cinéma* and the *Cinémathèque.**

The effect of the material (after fifty years in storage) was 'bewitching' ('enchantant'), Gerard Schlesinger writes in the *Cahiers du Cinéma*.

Auto exposure meant that the 35mm film material first developed in a series of outlines and incorrect colours. Through the subsequent development of the unexposed negatives in the film lab, shadows and echoes overlay these outlines and colours. Parts of the film were scratched and this damage gave it a *unique* character, in contradiction to the theories of Walter Benjamin. According to Schlesinger, the sound track possesses 'cruel beauty' or 'something like strength of character'. Richard Wagner should *always* be 'fragmented' in this way. The recording also includes the authentic noise track of the camera's operating sounds and the artillery and bomb detonations. This original sound, Schlesinger writes, this effect of 'being in medias res' adds rhythm to Wagner's music and makes it the PROPERTY of the twentieth century instead of an empty quotation from the nineteenth.

---

* Re-sequencing = image and sound are synchronized on the cutting table. She mixed together the 17.5mm perforated film with the peculiar fragments of music to make a single version. Otherwise it would not have been possible to synchronize the visual recordings with the much longer sound recordings, she said. She adhered to the descriptions noted on the film canisters. She herself spoke not a single word of German, but had an acquaintance at the Goethe Institute in Paris with whom she slept from time to time.

The camera and the tripod are visible in some of the film as well as the sound recording equipment. The 'prompts of the souffleuse have the high-pitched timbre of Ufa sound pictures. The pitch of voices in the talkies of that time would seem therefore not to be a result of the actors' speech training, but rather of the conventions of sound recording.'

It was a mistake, according to Schlesinger, to mix the fragments of music together. This creates—in contrast to the original recordings—a BAD OVERALL SOUND. Mixing the music can only document the *intention* of those who made the recording, not what they actually *did*: the whole point, Schlesinger writes, is this ingenious discovery, namely, the BEAUTY OF FRAGMENTS.

Thanks to the intervention of *Cahiers du Cinéma*, the three thousand metres of film and innumerable fragments of music are played in a total of 103 separate sections. Every portion of film has just one sound track allotted to it. Where there is no visual material, cinema-goers experience a concert without pictures. At the suggestion of *Cahiers du Cinéma*, Nono's agent added the work to his catalogue. It is not only the scores that an individual writes that count as finished works, but also the musical gems an individual discovers and preserves. Yes, it is an art in itself to procure such treasure. I myself could never have imagined such a telephone box voice, says Nono's agent, let alone one with such expressive power. This work of the twentieth century in images and sound is absolutely unique. 'Property is the good fortune of finding, once in a lifetime, such a treasure.'

Outline of a scene:
They sat at the back of the projection room in the film lab of the Cinétyp company in Paris. Together they were supposed to draw up a protocol of the re-sequenced samples (sound and images combined). It was a matter of quality control.

—Filament bulbs on the cellar roof can be seen to shine over everything and pocket torches illuminate the music stands.

—The walls shine as well.

—Yes. The pocket torches are replaced from time to time.

—When the batteries have to be changed. You can see that some of the bulbs have already become dimmer.

—The faces are in shadow.

—Yes, but the vigorous movements of the musicians move the shadows, so that something 'ghostly' keeps the room in movement, an impression of 'hard-working figures'.

—Clouds of dust waft down past the lights. Those are the hits of artillery shells.

—Or bomb detonations.

—Yes.

—The dust has to be cleaned off the instruments. More often than at rehearsals in the Opera. Look over there: the brass section, stopping to polish their instruments. Dust and spit combined.

—And now this section has to jump to bar 486?

—Exactly. That way they are playing together with the strings again and the individual singing voices that we can hear over the loud speakers via the two-way radio from the neighbouring cellar.

—Would you say that it sounds 'scratchy'?

—Only in the way that army messaging devices always sound. The artillery, if you listen carefully, also sounds tinny in the recording, so it must be a general problem with the sound quality.

—And here three of the seven parts of the orchestra are out of sync.

—Just like in the churches of the High Middle Ages. Musical notes wander around the space available. There is no convergent 'harmony'.

—Although with the best will in the world, it's hard to consider two-way radios as a *qualified* space. Here all you can see is a telephone line with loud speakers directly attached by cable. It's more like a kind of anti-cathedral.

—But it works all the better as an imagined space.

—Better in what way?

—Think of the actual situation. At any moment one of the other rehearsal cellars (or perhaps your own) could sustain a direct hit and collapse. Then you would only hear the noise of catastrophe. Imagination is determined by an actual situation.

—So it's not so much the sound of a space, but of a cage?

—Absolutely: the collective noise of many spaces. A new kind of habitat meaning that at last, just for once, music is in sync with reality. It can't be achieved by setting up a symphony orchestra in a factory and pretending it is a venue for symphony concerts. That only makes the factory unreal, which is no way to make the music more real. But here, in dire straits, in besieged Vienna, a new sound space for real music is created: the resurgence of music out of the spirit of contemporary history. The spaces are the message. In the ak-ak sounds of the musical notes I hear the starry sky at night. Something pure, clear.

—Do you think that was what Wagner envisaged?

—I do indeed.

—He didn't belong to the twentieth century though.

—Timeless genius makes a habit of seizing on anything of musical value. Hear that? That's the fourth group of brass players with one *timpano* and three *celli* from the right side of the orchestra. It sounds just like Giacomo Meyerbeer, *La Juive,* fifth act, first scene. That's where

Wagner had it from, and here, in the right space, it reverts to Meyerbeer. Music doesn't allow itself to be expropriated.

—It sounds 'interesting'.

—'Entrancing'. The right expression.

—It's dark now.

—Yes, a series of detonations close by has destroyed the electric cable. Some of the pocket torches are lying on the ground. Look, infantry soldiers are running up the cellar steps to reconnect the electricity supply. Some things are still visible with the help of the pocket torches that have been fixed onto the music stands again. And there's candlelight, a candelabrum with twelve candles as general lighting. Useless for reading the music on the individual stands but comforting for the room as a whole. There's the conductor coming in. He gives the first violins and the two singers whispered instructions. He is carrying a basket with twelve new torches and food.

—The other cellars know nothing about the momentary fall-out of this group of musicians?

—On the contrary. The message is passed on by radio. Over on the left you can see a *Wehrmacht* radio operator. There are also prompters in each cellar. This one has a Hungarian accent and has been borrowed from the Opera.

—Wouldn't it have been better to play 'Rhine Gold' instead of 'Twilight of the Gods'? It would have been a more optimistic opening. Better as propaganda than a drama of downfall.

—People in Vienna were no longer prepared to exaggerate and could lie no longer. Those who organized the recordings were bereft, in despair.

—An unconscious artwork with claims to the truth?

—In so far as all efforts failed and something was created that no-one had intended. They never meant air raid shelters to become workshops of art.

—Hard to believe.

—A chance find. The main achievement lay in making this discovery in the cellars of the museum in Sotschi.

—Are there many such discoveries waiting to be made in the world?

—Many. You have to assume that for six thousand years now things were always being hidden or forgotten.

Lenin and Demel

Anton Kuh

Bolshevism stands at Vienna's gates, Bela Kun has unfurled his banner; between the Opera and the Grand Hotel, beggars in soldiers' uniform display their prosthetic limbs in the April sunshine for all to see; one lame and one blind man reel around together like characters from a fairytale, making the streets resound with their piercing lament: 'Two poor invalids...'

The rags of an ersatz wartime existence still hang from the city. But what has become of its feudal lords? Harrach and Hardegg and Kinsky and Trautmannsdorff?

Even if they had to eat sawdust, they would still rather repair to Konditorei Demel—their beloved refuge on the Kohlmarkt—than to any arcadia of abundance frequented by common folk. Thankfully, though, ices and cream puffs and waffles are still to be had there. Highly decorative delicacies, perfumed variations on the rationing laws.

The serving ladies are still courteous, respectful and dignified, like sisters from an aristocratic convent. They combine the allure of Wilbrandt-Baudius, grande dame of the Burgtheater, with the discreet devotion of a theatre attendant. Their faces show the concern they feel at the changed times that threaten to do away with princes, barons, society beaux, and single women alike. What kind of a world would it be without the pleasures of serving and thanking, without the glamorous backdrop of the nobility, without the recompense of a jovial remark from the lips of a count? The Demel waitresses have a sense of belonging to the *haute volée* that is more intense and more intimate than that of Xandi Kinsky, Dolfi Starhemberg, or Taschkerl Auersperg. They might as well sport memorial medallions for Old Austria on their black blouses.

That beloved, unforgettable country finds its final culinary resting place here.

Although everything else has been shaken to its foundations, Sister Thesa stands firm. Her kiss on the hand of an aristocrat remains the most spontaneous and legitimate endorsement of the *ancien régime*.

A dialect that is otherwise extinct is still to be heard at Demel. Known as 'knautschen' and also often heard at the races, it is characterized by resignation: having squeezed sounds through the nose and over the palate, the speaker leaves them to find their own way out, regardless of whether or not they join together to form sentences. Effortlessness is, of course, the foremost distinction of the aristocracy; His Royal Highness neither emphasizes nor articulates, otherwise one might think he wanted something, even if it were just—to be in the right. That's why Austria's aristocrats developed their own language, nonchalance as intonation: the tongue lies back indolently as though in a club armchair, the vowels are given a little injection of perfumed boredom from the narrowed nasal cavity, the 'r's are picked up by the palatal plate as though they were the crumbs of a delicate tart, the lips barely part so as to take in no more air than is absolutely necessary from the common domain—and these resonant rations are consumed morsel by morsel, crumbled into a sauce of mocking smiles.

This was the language spoken by the top hundred who used to divide up between them the profits of 'Austria' Ltd; it is Demel-prose.

The count still wears a monocle and carelessly scoffs sugared dough balls as though he were plucking grapes from a bunch. Asks: 'Did the Bolsheviks already call by?' (Sounds like 'cawl byy-yy'.)

The sisters in chorus: 'teeheehee!'

'No, my Lord Count.'

'There's time yet, my Lord Count.'

'We don't mind waiting a little longer, my Lord Count.'

'Teeheehee!'

'I was so scared already, don't you know—I'm the fearful type. Run along, Thesa, won't you?—bring me an ice. Hallo there, Pauckerl—tell me, how's Aunt Cl'thild'?'

'Oh, she was just over at Hansi Palffy's.'

'She scared of the Bolsheviks too?'

'Dashed if she ain't. Alexander says she don't dare leave the house anymore—'cos of the Bolsheviks, he says.'

'Yes, well, as you can see, we're all so scared, what?'

'Teehee!'

The ghost of Demel 1919: Lenin sits between every portion of ice cream and a member of the House of Gotha. They try to exorcise him with wit and mockery. But shivers run down their spine. They sing loudly to themselves as they walk further into the dark wood of the changing times…and as death taps them on the shoulder—'come, little brother!'—they respond with mild embarrassment: '*dégoûtant!*'

Oh Happy Eyes*

In memoriam Georg Groddeck

Ingeborg Bachmann

It started with 2.5 in the right eye and 3.5 in the left, Miranda remembers, but now, harmoniously, she has 7.5 diopters in each eye. That means the near point of her vision has moved abnormally close, the far point as well. She did once think she should learn her prescription off by heart, just in case she needed to have new glasses made unexpectedly, after an accident or somewhere away from home. She gave that idea up, though, because the specifications are complicated by the fact that she also suffers from blurred vision, and this second deformation alarms

* The title is a quotation from Goethe, *Faust II*.

her as she can never quite understand why her meridians are defective and don't have the same refractive power at any point. Even the expression 'astigmatism' seems to bode ill, and she says to Josef in self-important tones: astigmatism, it's worse than being blind, you know.

Sometimes, however, Miranda has the feeling that her ailing optical systems are a 'gift from heaven'. She is quick to proffer such exclamations, attributing them to heaven, God and the saints—yes, they are a gift, even if only an inherited one. For it never ceases to amaze her how other people can bear all the things they see and have to see every day. But perhaps they do not suffer so very much after all, as they have no other system for perceiving the world. Perhaps people who see normally, including those with normal astigmatism, have been totally numbed, and maybe there is no reason for Miranda to carry on feeling that she has been granted an unfair privilege, a mark of distinction.

Surely Miranda would not love Josef any less if she had to see his yellowish, discoloured teeth every time he laughed. She knows what these teeth look like from close up, but the possibility of 'always seeing' them makes her uncomfortable. And she probably wouldn't be bothered by the shock of seeing the wrinkles around his eyes on the days when he's tired, either. Nevertheless, she prefers to be spared such detailed insight and is glad that her feelings cannot be threatened or weakened by it. And besides, as she receives messages on other wavelengths anyway, she notices in the bat of an eyelid whether Josef is tired, why he's tired and whether he's laughing out of high spirits or irritation. She doesn't need to have him in front of her in clear focus as others do, she doesn't examine people, doesn't take photos of them with spectacle lenses, but instead paints them in her own way, based on her own impressions, and Josef at least came out very well for her from the start. She fell in love with him at first glance, although every optician would shake his head as Miranda's first glances can only ever result in catastrophic errors. But she stands by her first glance, and of all men, Josef—whether in the early sketches or later more detailed versions, in light or in shade—is the one with whom Miranda is really rather satisfied.

With the help of a tiny corrective measure—a diverging lens—with a golden spectacle frame slid over her nose, Miranda can see into hell. This inferno has never ceased to lose its horrors for her. That's why, always on her guard, she looks warily around restaurants before putting her glasses on to read the menu, or up and down the street when she wants to hail a cab, for if she is not careful, things move into her field of vision that she will never be able to forget: she sees a crippled child or a dwarf or a woman with an amputated arm, but such figures are in actual fact only the most glaring, the most striking in the midst of an accumulation of unhappy, taunting, damned faces marked by humiliation or crime, visages you could never dream up. And their effluence, this all-pervasive emanation of hideousness, brings tears to her eyes, makes her lose the ground under her feet, and to stop that happening, she reads the menu swiftly and tries to tell a taxi from a private car as quick as a flash, and then she puts her glasses away again, all she needs is a little bit of information. She doesn't want to know any more than that. (Once, to punish herself, she walked around Vienna for a whole day with her glasses on, through several districts, and she doesn't believe it would be right to repeat this walk. It would take more strength than she has, and she needs her whole strength to deal with the world that she knows.)

Miranda's excuses for not recognizing people or failing to acknowledge their greetings are not always taken seriously, some dismiss them as silly or else believe them to be a particular form of arrogance. Stasi says almost viciously:

Well, put your glasses on, then!

No, no way, never, Miranda answers, I couldn't bear it. Would you wear glasses?

Stasi retorts:

Me? Why should I? My sight is quite decent, thank you.

Decent, Miranda thinks, what does that mean, decent? And somewhat diffidently she pursues the subject: but if someone didn't want to for reasons of vanity, would that be something you could understand?

Stasi doesn't give Miranda an answer, which means: not just unbelievably arrogant, but vain as well, and to top it all, the unbelievable luck she always has with men if what they say is true, but it's no use trying to get anything out of the reserved Josef.

To Josef, Miranda says: Stasi is much more relaxed now, she was never as nice as this before, I think she must be in love, whatever it is, it's doing her good. What is it that he actually wants from her now, divorce and the child? I just don't get it, the whole story.

Josef is preoccupied, as though he doesn't really know who she's talking about. But yes of course, he agrees, Stasi has become much pleasanter company, almost bearable, maybe it's due to Berti's medical skill or even thanks to Miranda and all the rest of them; before, Stasi had simply been run down, exhausted, all her misfortunes had made her quite obnoxious, but now she's going to get custody of the child after all. This is news to Miranda, and she's hearing it from Josef. She immediately wants to ring Stasi and congratulate her, then she is seized by a momentary chill, she checks to see if the window is open but it's closed, Josef has his nose in the newspaper again, Miranda looks at the roof of the house opposite. How dark it is in this street, the houses are all too expensive and too dark, built on a place of execution from the good old days.

Miranda has been waiting in an Arabia Espresso bar, now it's time to go, she pays, bangs her head against the glass door of the bar, rubs her forehead, that'll come up in another big bruise, the last bump has only just gone down, she could really do with some ice straight away, but where is she supposed to get ice from right now? Glass doors are more hostile than people, for Miranda never stops hoping that people will look after her, like Josef does, and she's already smiling trustingly at the pavement again. Maybe she's mistaken though because first Josef wanted to go to the bank and then to the book shop or was it the other way round, and so she stands on the Graben and tries to find him among all the other people crossing the Graben and then she takes up position in Wollzeile with bleary, straining eyes. She looks towards Rotenturmstrasse and then towards Parkring,[*] first she thinks he must be close by, then far off, ah, there he is now, coming from Rotenturmstrasse after all, and she is overjoyed at the prospect of a total stranger, who is however abruptly released from her affections as soon as he is identified as Not-Josef. Then the anticipation begins again, grows more intense, and finally, although delayed, there is a kind of sunrise in her misty

---

[*] All of these names are exclusive shopping streets in Vienna's first district.

world, the veil is torn in two, Josef is there, she takes his arm and walks on happily.

Despite everything, this veiled world, in which Miranda wants just one particular thing—namely Josef—is the only world in which she feels at ease. She will never accept the more precise world, graciously granted to her by Vienna's foremost glasses boutique—a foreign rival of Söhnges and Götte[*]—whether it be made of leaded glass, light glass, or plastic, or else seen through the most modern of contact lenses. She does make an effort, she tries, has to stop trying unexpectedly, gets a headache, tears in her eyes, has to lie in a darkened room, and once, before the Opera Ball,[**] but really only as a surprise for Josef, she had those expensive contact lenses sent from Munich, with the advertising slogan on the invoice that read: *always look on the bright side*. Bent over a black cloth she tried to put the tiny things in—memorizing the instructions, blinded by the anaesthetic eye drops—and then one of the lenses got lost in the bathroom after all, never to be found again, it leapt down the plughole in the shower or else shattered on the tiles and the other slid under Miranda's eyelid, high up over the eyeball. Despite all the storms of tears, nothing helped until Berti arrived and it

[*] Now defunct, but at the time Bachmann was writing, Austria's main indigenous optician.

[**] The annual ball held at the Vienna State Opera, the grandest social event of the Viennese calendar, which attracts international VIPs and class war campaigners alike.

took another hour after that despite Berti's expert fingers, nothing, Miranda doesn't care to remember now how long it took until Berti was able to find the lens and remove it, and she still protests from time to time: at least I did everything I could.

Even Josef sometimes forgets when he speaks to her that, although he is not dealing with a blind woman as such, she is nevertheless a borderline case and doesn't really know much about things that are very well known; nevertheless, her uncertainty is productive. Although she looks hesitant, she is not frail but self-reliant, precisely because she knows exactly what is brewing in the jungle where she lives, and because she is ready for anything. As Miranda cannot be corrected, reality has to put up with the temporary changes she imposes on it. She makes things bigger, smaller, tells tree shadows and clouds where to go, admires two mouldy green lumps because she knows they must be the Karlskirche, and in the Vienna Woods, she sees the woods not the trees, breathes deeply, tries to get her bearings.

Look over there, Bisamberg!*

---

* Bisamberg is the last in the chain of hills that make up the ridge of the Vienna Woods, the only peak to be situated to the north-east rather than south-west of the Danube. Leopoldsberg is a peak in the Vienna Woods on the western bank of the river.

It's only Leopoldsberg, but that doesn't matter. Josef is patient. Where did you put your glasses this time?—Oh, I must have left them in the car by mistake. But why shouldn't it be Bisamberg, just for a change? Miranda asks herself and pleads with Leopoldsberg, one of these days, to do her the favour of being the right peak.

Affectionate and trusting and always half nestled into Josef's gauntness, she tackles the next tree root that obstructs the footpath. 'Affectionate' is not just the way she feels right now, everything about Miranda is affectionate, from her voice to her tentative footsteps, including her entire function in the world, which must surely be quite simply that of showing affection.

When Miranda gets into a tram in Vienna, she sways between the other passengers in an AK or a BK* without noticing that the conductor and the old lady with the wrong ticket are motivated by pure hatred, that those pushing their way onto the tram are infested with rabies and those who are about to get off have murder in their eyes, and when Miranda has made her way to the 'Exit' with many apologies, happy that she recognized Schottenring in time and can get down two steps without help, she thinks that people are all 'very nice indeed', actually, and the other people on the AK tram who get off to go to

* Until the 1980s, the names of the trams going around the Ring.

the university probably have no idea why the mood is suddenly better and the air breathable once more, only the conductor realizes that someone has forgotten to take their change, probably that woman who got off at the stock exchange or at Schottenring. The good-looking one. Nice legs. He pockets the money.

Miranda often loses things where others have something taken from them, and she walks past people unscathed instead of colliding with them. When she does collide with them, then it's a mistake, a completely chance occurrence, her fault entirely. She could have masses read for all the car drivers who haven't run her over, light a candle to St Florian for every day that her apartment doesn't go up in flames due to the lit cigarettes she puts down somewhere, looks for and then, praise be, finds again, even though there's already a hole burnt in the table.

It is sad, perhaps, just a little sad, how many stains, burn marks, overheated cooking rings and ruined saucepans there are in Miranda's apartment. But each time, there's a happy ending, and when Miranda opens up because the bell rings and there's an unexpected stranger on the doorstep, she is always very lucky. It's Uncle Hubert, it's her old friend Robert, and she throws her arms around Uncle Hubert or Robert or whoever it is. It could of course have been a beggar or a burglar, that thuggish Novak, or the serial killer of women who is still at large in the first district, but Miranda is only ever visited by her best friends in the Blutgasse.[*] The tingling presence or debatable absence of all the other people—the ones that a not unsociable Miranda fails to recognize at large gatherings, parties, at the theatre, or in concerts—surrounds her at all times. It's just that she doesn't know whether it's Dr Bucher waving to her or perhaps not, and it could also have been Herr Langbein, given the height and circumference. She comes to no conclusion. In a world of alibis and surveillance, Miranda puzzles—not over the mystery of the universe, of course, over nothing of particular importance. Nevertheless: does that silhouette want to be or not to be Herr Langbein? It remains an enigma. Where others seek clarity, Miranda holds back, no, that's not her ambition, and where others sense secrets, behind their backs and behind everyone and everything, there's only one secret for Miranda and it's on the side that is facing her. A distance of two metres is enough and already the world is inscrutable, other human beings are inscrutable.

Hers is the most relaxed face to be found at the Musikverein,[**] an oasis of peace in a hall in which she has been seen by at least twenty gesticulating persons and has not

---

[*] A residential street at the heart of the oldest part of Vienna's first district, literally 'Blood Alley'.
[**] Vienna's most famous concert hall, location of the New Year's Concert.

seen any one at all herself. She has learned not to be nervous in rooms in which people take note of each other, weigh up, write down, write off, avoid, eye up. She doesn't dream, she is simply at rest. Others seek peace of mind, Miranda has peace of eye. Her gloves quietly take on a life of their own and fall under her seat. Miranda feels something on her leg, she fears that she has mistakenly rubbed against the leg of her neighbour, she murmurs: so sorry. The leg of a chair has fallen in love with Miranda. Josef picks up the concert programme, Miranda smiles uncertainly and tries to hold her legs strictly together and straight. Dr Bucher, who is not Herr Langbein but Herr Kopetzky, sits three rows behind her in a huff, trying to find an explanation for the fickleness of this woman for whom he once would have given almost anything, but really anything—

Josef asks:

Have you got your glasses with you?

But of course, Miranda says, and digs around in her handbag. She has the feeling that she brought gloves with her as well, but she'd better not mention that to Josef, no, her glasses, that's strange, must be in the bathroom after all or by the door or in the pocket of her other coat or, Miranda just can't understand it, but she quickly says:

No, I'm afraid I don't. But I don't need to see anything at a concert anyway.

Josef says nothing, moved by his Miranda leitmotif: my artless angel.

For Miranda other women have no defects, they are creatures who have no hair on either their upper lips or legs, who are always perfectly coiffed, devoid of enlarged pores or impurities, without spots or nicotine-yellow fingers, no, she is the only one, fighting alone against her imperfections before the shaving mirror which once belonged to Josef, and in which she sees things that she hopes Josef will have the goodness to overlook. Afterwards though, when Miranda has finished her exercises in self-criticism, she stands in front of the forgiving Biedermeier mirror in the bedroom and considers herself 'passable', 'alright', it's not so bad, and she's wrong there as well but, after all, Miranda lives in the midst of a dozen different ways of deceiving herself, her life hangs in the balance between the most and the least favourable every day.

On good days, Miranda has three pairs of glasses: a pair of gold-frame prescription sunglasses with black inlay, a light, transparent, cheap pair to wear at home and a reserve pair with a loose lens that she has been told doesn't suit her. And anyway, it must have been made to an earlier prescription, for Miranda sees everything 'wrong' when she's wearing her 'reserve'.

There are days when all three pairs are nowhere to be found, vanished, lost, and then Miranda doesn't know what to do. Josef comes from Prinz-Eugen-Strasse before eight o'clock in the morning and turns the entire apartment upside down, he loses his temper with Miranda, he suspects the cleaning lady and the workmen, but Miranda knows that nobody steals, it's all her fault, of course. As Miranda cannot tolerate reality, but cannot function without some points of reference, from time to time reality mounts little retaliation campaigns against her. Miranda understands this, she nods like a conspirator to the objects making up the backdrop that surrounds her, and on days like these the funny crease that she has, where she doesn't need to have one yet, from screwing up her eyes and opening them extra wide, gets even deeper. Josef promises to go to the opticians straight away, for Miranda can't exist without glasses and she thanks him, clutching him with sudden fear and wanting to say something, but not just because he came to help her, but because he helps her to see and to carry on seeing. Miranda doesn't know what's wrong with her, and she wants to say, help me, please! And thinks, out of the blue, after all, she's more attractive than I am.

During the week in which Miranda has to wait and can't go out and loses the overview, Josef has to go out to dinner twice with Anastasia to advise her on her divorce. After the first time, Stasi rings her the next morning, after the second time she doesn't ring any more.

Yes, we went to the 'Römischer Kaiser'. Dreadful. Bad, the food had been bad, and she'd felt cold all evening.

And Miranda can't get a word out in reply because for her the 'Römischer Kaiser' is the most beautiful and the best place in Vienna, because that was where she first went out to dinner with Josef and now all of a sudden it is the most dreadful—Miranda are you listening? Well then, as I was just saying. Afterwards we went on to the Eden Bar. Frightful. The clientele!

There must be a particular meaning behind Stasi's way of saying clientele, but what could that be? Miranda breathes more easily now. She's never been to the Eden Bar with Josef, which affords her a scrap of comfort. Is she just pretending or is this how she really is?

Stasi assures her, after a further half hour of elaboration: in any case, you didn't miss anything.

Miranda wouldn't have put it that way, 'missed nothing', for she is afraid of missing everything at the moment. The week seems endless, and every day brings another evening when something stops Josef from coming round. Then the glasses are ready, just a few hours later he brings them round from the opticians, but it happens again straight away. Miranda is beside herself, she has to lie down, wait, and calculate how long it will take Josef to get back to his Prinz-Eugen-Strasse. She finally manages to get hold of him, she doesn't know how to begin telling him that the new glasses fell into the sink.

Yes, just imagine, into the hand basin. I feel like an invalid, I can't go out, I can't see anyone. You understand.

From the fourth district, Josef says:

A fine mess. But you've often gone out without glasses before.

Yes but. Miranda can't come up with anything convincing. Yes but, it's different now, because usually I have them in my pocket, at least.

Oh come on, no you don't!

Don't let's because of that, whispers Miranda, please, you sound so.

I sound so what?

So different. Just different.

And because there is no reply, she says quickly:

No, I will come after all, dear, I just feel so uncertain, yesterday I nearly, yes, nearly but not quite, fainted, really, it's quite horrible, I was trying the reserve pair. Everything 'wrong', distorted. But you understand.

When Josef is silent like this he has not understood.

Unfortunately I can't see the logic in it, says the different sounding Josef, and hangs up.

Miranda sits by the telephone, guilty. Now she's even given Josef a reason, but for what? Why do my glasses fall into the washbasin, why is Josef and why is the world, oh

God, it's just not possible. Is there not another restaurant in the whole of Vienna? Does Josef have to go to the 'Römischer Kaiser' with her? Does Miranda have to cry, does she have to live in a pitch-dark cave, to stagger along the bookshelves pressing her face into the backs of the books and then even to find a book *De l'Amour*. After she has read the first twenty pages with great effort she feels dizzy, slips further down in her chair, the book on her face, and tips forward with the chair onto the floor. The world has turned black.

As she knows that the glasses did not fall into the sink by chance, as she needs must lose Josef and would prefer to lose him of her own free will, she begins to take action. She rehearses the first few steps towards a conclusion that she will arrive at one day in a blind panic. Josef and Anastasia must never suspect that she is causing them to drift towards each other, Stasi in particular, which is why Miranda needs to invent a story for all of them which is bearable and more appealing than what is actually happening: the main thing is never to have been interested in Josef in the first place, really; she begins to practise this part straight away. Josef is a very dear, old friend, nothing more, and she will be pleased, she will also claim to have always had an inkling. The only thing that she will not have suspected is what the two of them are really up to and are planning, how far they have already gone and the end that they are about to inflict on her. Miranda rings Ernst, and he, emboldened, rings her back a few days later. She makes several mysterious comments, and then half confessions to Stasi: Ernst and I, that's not the way it is, no, who says that? No, it was never really over, I mean, after all, I can tell you, can't I, always more than just one of the usual affairs that everyone has, you understand—

And she murmurs something more, as though she has already said too much. Confused, Anastasia discovers that Miranda just can't forget darling Ernst, and it's just typical that no one in this benighted city, where everyone is supposed to know everything about everyone, has the slightest clue.

Miranda contrives to meet up with Stasi but still to be seen in time with Ernst by the entrance, where she begins to kiss the hesitant bashful Ernst, asking him between kisses and excited laughter whether he can still remember how to unlock the front door to her house.

Stasi discusses the front door scene in detail with Josef. She saw everything quite clearly. Josef doesn't have much to say on the subject, he really doesn't want to mull over a Miranda in darling Ernst's arms by the front door with Anastasia. Josef is convinced that he is the only man in Miranda's life, but the next day, after he has made Anastasia breakfast, he is quite amused by the whole thing. He doesn't find it so bad any more, a relief even, and after all, Anastasia is so very clever and insightful. He will have to get used to the idea that Miranda needs other men, that Ernst is a better match for her when all is said and done, because of their shared interests apart from anything else, and he can even imagine her with Berti or with Fritz, who only talks about her in that horrible way because he never got anywhere with her and would jump at the chance if only she wanted him. For Josef Miranda has new powers of attraction that he hadn't noticed before, and, as Anastasia starts to talk about it once again, he proudly begins to believe that Miranda is capable of causing real havoc.

Poor Fritz, that was when he started to drink.

Josef is not as sure about this as Anastasia, because Fritz had already been fond of the bottle before. And once he even defends Miranda half-heartedly. Stasi is dissecting Miranda's character, claiming above all that she doesn't have one, after all she changes all the time. First you see her all elegant in the theatre, and then she's unkempt again, a skirt with ragged edges or hair not done for weeks. Josef says:

But you don't understand. It all depends on whether she has just found her glasses or not and then it all depends on whether she puts them on or not.

That stupid woman, Stasi thinks, he is still hung up on her, no, I'm the stupid woman, because I think I've got hopes of angling Josef and now he doesn't know what he wants, what does he want? But it's as clear as day, he wants that cunning, slovenly, stupid, that—here Stasi runs out of adjectives—she's got him totally under her thumb with her helplessness, Josef wants to protect, and who's going to protect me?

And she cries two tears into her orange juice from her beautiful, blue eyes that see decently and swears to herself that she will never cry again her whole life, at least not this year, and not over Josef.

Josef's blessed Miranda, the patron saint of all border-line cases, is roasted, quartered, put on a spit and burnt alive by Stasi, and Miranda feels it bodily although she will never hear a single word of it. She doesn't trust herself to go out of the house any more, sits there with another new pair of glasses—she doesn't want to go out into the street. Ernst comes round for tea, and they make plans to go to the Salzkammergut, and Berti comes round once to check up on her, he thinks she has a vitamin deficiency. Miranda looks at him trustingly, that's her belief too, absolutely, and she suggests to Berti herself that she should eat lots of raw carrots. Filling up a long prescription form with writing, Berti says:

Apart from anything else, they're good for your eyes.

Miranda says gratefully:

Of course, and you know that my eyes are the most important thing to me.

But she can hardly bear to look at Josef now. Instead, she looks past him, slightly to the right or left or somewhere else, so that her gaze is vacant. She would prefer to put her hand over her eyes, for her greatest temptation is still to stare raptly at Josef the whole time. Instead of her heart, her stomach, or her head, as would be the case with other women, the charade he is playing quite simply hurts her eyes, they have to bear all the pain, because seeing Josef was the most important thing in the world to her. And every day now, the following happens: seeing Josef less. Seeing less of Josef.

Miranda puts ice cubes into Josef's glass, and Josef lounges around as though nothing had changed, except he talks about Stasi all the time as though they had always talked about Stasi. Sometimes he says 'Anastasia', with ceremonial solemnity. Wherever he is, Josef is in Miranda's way, she looks at her manicured fingernails. 'Porcelain', that was the nail varnish that accompanied the Josef Era, but now that Josef only ever kisses her hand fleetingly on arrival and departure, and no longer admires and studies 'porcelain', perhaps she can do without the nail colour now as well. Miranda jumps up, closes the window. She is oversensitive to noise. Lately there has been nothing but noise in this city—radios, televisions, young dogs yapping, and those little delivery vans, yes, it brings Miranda up with a jolt, heavens, she can't start wishing to hear poorly as well! And even then she would still be able to hear the noises loud and clear, but would not be able to hear the voices that she most likes to hear with the same clarity anymore.

Miranda says pensively:

I'm an ear person, I have to like the sound of somebody's voice, otherwise it'll never lead to anything.

But doesn't she always say that she only likes beautiful people? Nobody knows more beautiful people than Miranda, she attracts them, for she puts beauty above every other quality. If she is left, and Josef is in the process of leaving her, then it will be because Anastasia is more beautiful, or particularly beautiful. It's the explanation for all the ups and downs in Miranda's life.

(You see, Berti? It's just that she's more beautiful than I am.)

But what has Josef been talking about all this time, oh, only about Stasi again, unless Miranda is much mistaken.

It's a very, very rare thing, Josef says.

Oh, do you think so? —Miranda still hasn't understood what he's talking about. She listens to him less and less.

Yes, he says, but with you it's possible.

So that's what he's building up to, and now Miranda looks at him directly for the first time in weeks. Oh yes, she will transform this dreadful deceit into truth. Doesn't he get it? Friendship—she and Josef, friends?

Well, says Miranda, it's not so very rare, friendship. And an internal, other, less sublime Miranda cannot contain herself: my God, how stupid this man is, he's too stupid for words, doesn't he get it at all, and will it be like this for all eternity, and why does the only man that I like have to be this way!

Naturally, they'll still go to the concert on Sunday together, Josef decrees *en passant*. Miranda doesn't find it natural anymore. But as Stasi has to go to her husband's on Sunday because of the child, to 'thrash it all out' one last time, she has one last Sunday left.

What, not Mahler's Fourth again? she says.

No, the Sixth, I already said. Do you still remember London? Yes, Miranda says, her trust returned, she will listen to Mahler one more time with Josef and Stasi will not be able to spoil a single tone or wrest Josef from her on the steps of the Musikverein, so long as she has to be away on Sunday, to thrash things out.

After the concert, Josef takes Miranda home and not as though it were the last time. He can't bring himself to say it, in a couple of weeks she'll have got the message, she's behaving very sensibly. He puts his shoes back on again slowly and searches for his tie, which he ties with an absent-minded expression, tugging it into place without once looking at Miranda. He pours himself a shot of Sliwowitz, stands at the window and looks down at the street sign, 'I. Blutgasse'. My artless angel. He takes Miranda in his arms for a moment, brushes his lips against her hair and is incapable of seeing or feeling anything other than the word 'Blutgasse'. Who is doing this to us? What are we doing to each other? Why do I have to do this? and he would really like to kiss Miranda, but he can't and instead all he does is think, the executions carry on, it's an execution, because everything I do is a misdeed, that's it, deeds are misdeeds. And his angel looks at him with wide-open eyes, keeps her eyes wide open, questioning, as though there must be one last thing about Josef to see, but at the last with an expression which destroys him even further, because it exonerates him and grants absolution. Because Josef knows that no one will ever look at him like this again, Anastasia included, he closes his eyes.

Miranda didn't notice the door falling shut, she only hears a garage door banging downstairs, shouting from a bar somewhere in the distance, drunks on the street, the signature tune to a radio programme, and Miranda doesn't want to live anymore among these noises, lights, and shadows, she only has one point of access to the world left, a thudding headache that keeps her eyes closed, eyes that had been open for too long. What on earth was it that she saw last? Josef, that was it.

They meet again in Salzburg, in Café Bazar. Anastasia and Josef come in as a couple, and Miranda only trembles because Stasi looks so cross or so unhappy, whatever can the matter be, how am I supposed to—and Miranda, who always used to make a beeline for Josef, hears him say something mocking, something funny, at which point Stasi ploughs on towards her with a grim expression. Whereas Josef, fleeing, but surely not from her? has to go and say hello to old Hofrat Perschy, and then to the Altenwyls and all that clique, Miranda stands up with a jolt in her sandals and makes a beeline for the wan Stasi instead and murmurs, with a hint of red in her face, after she has kissed Stasi's cheek, reddened from hypocrisy and the effort of will she is making:

I'm so pleased for you, and for Josef as well, of course, yes, the postcard, thanks, yes, I got it.

Hello there Josef, she gives him her hand briefly, laughing, and Stasi says generously: Come on Josef, why don't you give Miranda a kiss?

Miranda pretends that she hasn't heard, she steps back, pulls Anastasia with her, hisses and whispers, redder and redder in the face, what do you know, Salzburg, so many people, what a dreadful coincidence, no, no, nothing bad, but I have to go straight off afterwards to pick up Ernst, surprise visit, you get it. Can you break it to Josef somehow, you'll say the right thing, I know.

Miranda is in a hurry, she only just has time to see that Anastasia nods sympathetically and looks 'sweet' all of a sudden, but also that she suddenly has the same red face. But perhaps it's just that she herself is so feverish that her sense of a stained world is getting the better of her. She's determined to make it back to the hotel though, despite her scarlet fever, despite this hot shame over her whole face and on her body, and she manages to see the double wing door, the only thing she doesn't see is that the wings of the door are not heading in the same direction as she is, but that one wing of the door is swinging against her, and as it flings her down in a hail of splintered glass and the impact and the blood that shoots out of her mouth and nose makes her even warmer, the last thing she thinks is: *always look on the bright side.*

Vienna

Heinrich Laube

For the second time, I was awoken by the dawn light shining on the Spinstress at the Cross.[*] Before me lay a gleaming sea of houses, the postillion cracked his whip and the conductor said with a satisfied smile: 'Look, your honour, there's Vienna'.

'Oho', I thought to myself, 'there's plenty of entertainment to be had here. There must be a thousand windows and more to look into, and—' Well, I wasn't sure exactly what else lay in store, but I was in a perfect fever of expectation.

---

[*] The 'Spinnerin Am Kreuz', a carved stone column dating from the fourteenth century, long marked Vienna's city boundary to the south and still stands today. Its name refers to the crusader's wife who set up her spinning wheel next to a simple stone cross to wait for her husband. When he finally returned, the couple donated the money she had earned to erect the elaborate Gothic monument.

It was still very early, and houseboys were sweeping the streets. Parlour maids slipped past the houses. Their shawls were so dainty that they didn't trouble themselves overly much to keep them on their bare shoulders. Cheeks still rosy from their slumbers, their clogs clattered at the end of smooth, white stockings. They laughed when they noticed your eyes on them. Everything was right with the world, the atmosphere was most diverting. Just from looking at the houses, you could tell that nothing but amusement was to be found inside. They have such an avuncular air, like good old friends who seek only to entertain and never complain about the bad times.

Every house in Vienna smiles cheerily. The smiles are those of older people who still like to enjoy themselves, though—not young, modern smiles, but cosy and welcoming. Not even the well-concealed government buildings are imposing, instead they seem to give a slight shrug of the shoulders and say: 'order must be kept, after all'; but they smile as well.

Although I hadn't even arrived at my inn, I could already tell how I would fare there. The city's aspect is not one of overwhelming beauty, but picturesque, charming, mellow. The warmer skies, the lilting speech, the plump, succulent bodies of the Viennese, their customs and habits, everything is locked in so blissful an embrace that the impulse is to open one's own arms wide. And in Vienna, no one opens them in vain. It is a supremely humane and accommodating place.

I will never forget my first Viennese morning. How quaint, how foolish my previous life seemed to me, with all its learning, its theories, its restless thoughts and constant struggle for independence. My God, I thought to myself on my arrival in Vienna, what is the good of all those muddle-headed things? Here is Greece, here is Classicism, seize the moment. Things are as they appear. They neither aim nor ask to mean anything more. They should be enjoyed. Here is true happiness on earth, put on your velvet coat and your white breeches, go out into the street, kiss the girls and eat fried chicken.—Let the affairs of the world pass you by. Books are bad for your digestion; thinking disturbs your sleep and your career.—I immersed myself in the bathtub, to wash away the man I used to be. Then I sat down to breakfast. Now, I thought to myself, you have truly arrived, like Alexander in Babylon. Now life and its joys can begin.

Breakfast in Vienna is like the foreword to one of those delightful novels we used to read so often in our youth. Like a child, the visitor looks forward to all the things the day will bring.

Next I betook myself to the nearest street corner.

Fortune smiled upon me: in letters as red as fire '*Sperl in floribus*' was emblazoned on the Rotenturmbastei:[*] '*Sperl in floribus*', '*Sperl in floribus*' murmured every passer-by, and pleasure sprang from face to face like a street urchin.—'*Sperl in floribus*' spread like wildfire from mouth to mouth, from street to street. Whenever two people exchanged a few words with each other, they took each other by the hand, saying 'Heute ist *Sperl in floribus!*'[**] A veritable horde of pleasure-seekers ran past me, buoyed up by these words, from Ferdinandsbrücke to Wieden.

Joyful faces illuminated the streets like chains of lights.

And I followed them over Stefansplatz, up Kärtnerstrasse as far as the Volksgarten and back again to the city wall. Everything in the Volksgarten and on the nearby city wall is tremendously clean, white and beautiful. A large building, just as white, stands close to the wall. It looks like dazzling official paper, inscribed with elegantly formed letters. This is Metternich's house. A little bridge connects it to the city wall, the imperial palace is ten paces further on. The prince can often be seen marching over this bridge, the portfolio for the preservation of Europe in his hand.

---

[*] A bastion that was an easterly part of the inner city walls, now Rotenturmstraße.
[**] 'Today, Sperl is "in flower"', i.e. open. 'Zum Sperl' was a tavern in the Leopoldstadt (today's second district) with a large pleasure garden where Strauss the Elder conducted dance music.

Strangely enough, the Volksgarten, garden of the people, is also close at hand. I had to admit to myself, though, that I had great good fortune in finding the most important people in town so swiftly. After Metternich, Sperl is the most important man in Vienna. The former is Minister for Foreign Affairs, the latter Minister of the Interior.

Upon hearing the name of Metternich, it has become a tradition among those German authors who look beyond the bounds of their own writing desks to spit out several expletives and to hold forth on freedom and tyranny.[*] To my way of thinking, Metternich is the greatest ruler of modern times, after Napoleon. I never cavil about greatness. I am a historian, and history without poetry is an abomination. Only one phenomenon exists that has but a single colour, and that is boredom. Metternich is a hero and demiurge in the same way as Achilles and Caesar, Alexander, and Napoleon Bonaparte. History judges not only principles but also deeds according to their singular weightiness. Absolutism was outmoded and under serious threat; Metternich nevertheless contrived to keep it in power despite all the storms that assailed it. He protected it against the irresistible, brilliant usurper Napoleon. He is

---

[*] Klemens Wenzel Fürst von Metternich, foreign minister of the Austrian Empire from 1809 until the revolutions of 1848, was one of the driving forces behind the reactionary peace settlement in Europe following the Napoleonic Wars.

the current god of absolutism. One must bow down to gods, even if one does not love them.

After Napoleon, I know of no male countenance more striking than that of Metternich. If anyone doesn't believe that Metternich rules Austria and half of Europe, the doubter need only visit a shop in Vienna selling art prints or the porcelain merchant's on Josefsplatz to be persuaded. And these are true portraits. The high yet yielding forehead, the proudly bulging eyes, the noble expression of the aristocratic nose and the fine, narrow lips; Metternich genuinely possesses all these Olympian features.

Metternich is perhaps the only man in Europe who knows that Christianity and every old faith came to an end with Luther. That is why Austria and Metternich have fought every kind of Protestantism to the death. For they rightly consider a half-hearted religion and half-hearted absolutism to be just as bad as irreligiousness and republic, they fear a chronic illness as much as an acute one.

I am very curious to see how my opinion of Vienna will develop, this city of paradise without fig leaf, serpent, or tree of knowledge. It is to be feared that I will have very favourable things to say about it, for my stomach was in an excellent state during my stay. I fear I will become a martyr, stay in Vienna and risk my intellect, liberalism, and Havana cigars, which are not to be had in Vienna.

But that's what makes Vienna Vienna; after a few weeks here you no longer need or miss anything that originates from elsewhere.

What is the reason for this, is it a highly developed culture or something else? Everything depends on finding an answer to this question. It is fundamental to a definition of Vienna and of our times. Staberl and I will do our best... *

The good old days and good old Vienna belong together like husband and wife. When you think of one, the other comes to mind. There is something touching about the fearful assiduousness with which the Viennese seek to uphold the belief that the good old days are still here in Vienna and that the city remains unchanged.

---

* 'Staberl' is a stock figure of traditional Viennese folk theatre, out of his depth as soon as he leaves his native city and liable to get into scrapes, but possessed of the native cunning needed to extricate himself—not unlike Mr Punch, although less obviously comic in his appearance.

The Feuilletonists

Ferdinand Kürnberger

'Have you read the charming feuilleton in today's news-paper?' the man opposite me at the *table d'hôte* asked his neighbour, a redoubtable citizen with imposing contours and a broad visage, which, just for a change, I shall com-pare to a well-stuffed, red velvet cushion instead of á full moon. 'Not I!' this gentleman responded, 'who on earth can be expected to read through all that stuff?'—'Come now, come now, Herr von Grammelmaier, I thought we had pretty good feuilletonists in Vienna now; I like them just as well as those of Paris or Berlin. They have a certain lightness of touch, a lively wit and don't take life too seriously...' 'That's as may be, but tell me, dear doctor, where are they to get their material from, their material! That's the *casus quaestionis*. The tower of the Stefansdom stays the same, the glacis, the city wall, Kohlmarkt and the Graben aren't going anywhere, we know all those "pictures of Vienna" or "scenes from Viennese life" or whatever they're all called inside out and backwards, with the best will in the world I couldn't think of a single new thing to add.'—'Come, come, Herr von Grammelmaier, after all, there are ten thousand households in the city and half a million souls; surely there's always something new to be discovered.'—'That's as may be, but just think of how many newspapers there are too, all looking for material, day by day, year in, year out. Every well runs dry eventually.' 'Excuse me, my dear sir!' I interjected, 'but to assume that a feuilletonist ever uses anything like the whole sum of material proffered by his location would be to seriously misjudge the situation. It would be a grave error. In the natural world the opposite is in fact the case. As, for example, the fish otter savours only the head of the trout and man nothing but the tail-end of the crayfish; as the goose, sheep, goat, cow, and horse search for different kinds of grazing on one and the same pasture; or else as the dogs of Constantinople, although they seem to live in the wildest kind of republic, are nevertheless kept in order by the strictest of internal police forces so that no dog is tempted, even by the juiciest of hambones, to cross the corner of his street into the territory of another dog—this is all *sans comparaison* of course—in exactly the same way, gentlemen, the natural history of the feuilletonist teaches us that this fine and civilized creature was created with an inherent respect for demarcation lines. Indeed, nature has organized this species in such a unique way and has assigned to it habitats so precisely defined that it affords a most congenial object of study to the thoughtful observer of microcosms. You, my dear sir, seem to conceive of the feuilletonist as a ravening, incontinent beast of prey, hunting down everything the city has to offer until hunger strikes due to lack of material: this type simply does not exist in the natural world or if it does, only as a debased form of the original genus. Generally speaking, the true feuilletonist affords us a much more varied and subtler embodiment of individuality's iridescent spectrum. He lives almost exclusively in the details. His natural habitat is specialization. Within the environment of the city, he marks off a particular territory for himself, and there—and only there—he finds his material and would continue to find it even if he lived as long as Nestor or Methuselah. To make myself clearer, I'd like to take the liberty of identifying a select few of the better-known species of the genus feuilleton.

'There is, for example, the common house feuilletonist, *Feuilletonistus domesticus.* Only look at this exemplar and you will see right away that there is actually no need for city or public life to provide inexhaustible subject matter for a feuilleton. The material of the house feuilletonist is just that, his house. He describes to us his staircase, his parlour, his furniture, the view from his window. We are acquainted with the moods of his cat and the philosophical worldview of his poodle. We know the precise spot behind the oven where his coffee machine stands, and when he takes up the cross of civilization every morning with the first cup of the day, we know how many beans he grinds, how many drops of spiritus he uses, how much water is in his milk and chalk in his sugar. Like Humboldt discussing the folds of the earth's crust, he talks about the tendency of his dressing gown to tear, missing buttons are sewn on before our eyes, in fact, he lives just like a prince whose every private action is performed in public. He seldom airs his own feelings (another aristocratic characteristic!), but shares with us in great historical detail the love affair between his poker and his shoe-horn, or else the stories he sees unfolding amongst the ornamental figures on his mantelpiece in the twilight hour.

'The light thrown on the main figure of such memoirs is mostly only glancing, however revealing it might be. Nonetheless, there is one aspect under which the aristo-cratic, nay, divine reserve of the house feuilletonist can be seen to have a very human side: in his great, historical conflicts with the concierge and the lame housemaid. The contrast that becomes apparent here between the spiritual

and material worlds, between culture and the natural
coarseness and despotism of unrefined elemental energy
would provide sufficient material in itself, of a timelessness
comparable to the millennial battles of the Iranians against
the Turanians or else the Dutch against the storm and
spring tides. And in actual fact, culture is often so sorely
tried in these conflicts that it seems from time to time as
though they must result in its absolute negation and anni-
hilation, that is to say, the house feuilletonist seems on the
verge of giving up and running away. But he never actually
resorts to this most drastic solution. The house feuilletonist has never been seen out in the open. At most, half of his
person leaves the confines of his home at times of insur-
mountable difficulty when he is moved to open his window and lean out. And behold, at that very moment, he
sees that the "Mercy" aria over there on the first floor (his
chronic affliction for years!) is moving out;[*] and, as he
looks and listens, the march from Tannhäuser resounds
from the garret on the right for the first time and the long,
long reign of terror during which the march from Rigo-
letto dominated the neighbourhood has finally come to an
end. But see there, over on the left in the bay window
behind the geraniums! Can it be possible? That darling

---

[*] From Giacomo Meyerbeer's opera *Robert le diable*, a smash hit throughout
Europe from its premiere in 1831 until the late nineteenth century.

little blonde head is, at last! showing itself for the first time without the dragon spinster at its side—whose austere guardianship had rendered psychographic study through the window pane impossible for so long. Oh, these are happy alterations indeed, so much so that they will give the house feuilletonist subject matter for a whole series of the most light-hearted, entertaining feuilletons!

'A contrast, or to put it more precisely, the diametrical opposite of the house feuilletonist is the street feuilletonist, *F. forensis*, in high German "flaneur", in low German— somewhat insensitively—"loafer". Exemplars of this species can often be found in front of the window displays of the larger fancy goods and fashion emporia. They also loiter in doorways to let the architecture of the magnificent new buildings opposite "work" on them; unfortunately, prestigious edifices freshly built in Vienna cannot be enjoyed from any other point of view. The street feuilletonist is the very soul of trade and industry. For, due to the incorrigible tendency of the average citizen not to believe their own eyes, luxurious "vaults" that swallow up thousands in rent or vast advertisements costing hundreds have no actual effect at all; the public is not electrified until the street feuilletonist has dashed off a casual word in his genteel, reserved manner about the "really rather pretty" trifles he happened to see here and there. "A nameless

longing then is waking"[*] in the tender heart of the young
female who, as recompense for entrusting her beautiful
earthly shell to a filthy rich old "codger", demands an
impressive inventory of earthly shells in return. A single
epithet in the feuilleton of newspaper X or Y—entrancing,
tasteful, delicate, quite charming—causes sleepless nights,
heavy accounts and every now and then, a feverish fluctu-
ation of the exchange rates. And so the street feuilletonist
strolls through the Hyde Park of modern industry like the
serpent in paradise, seducing at every step the modern
daughters of Eve who would much rather have the latest
style in Parisian fig leaves than the most dewy-eyed innocence in all eternity. In return, the street feuilletonist
himself is also constantly subjected to the gravest temptations. On the other side of the enormous, crystal-clear
shop windows, the managers of larger establishments lie
in wait for his wallet, not to empty but to fill it, and
in return to snare one of his magic words—entrancing,
tasteful, delicate, quite charming—which in the elegant
feuilleton of a widely-read newspaper can have such
"sense-robbing, heart-maddening power".[**] But "virtue is
more than a shade or a word / men may exercise its use on

---

[*] Quotation from Friedrich Schiller's 'Lied der Glocke' (Song of the Bell,
1799).
[**] Quotation from 'Die Kraniche des Ibykus' (The Cranes of Ibycus, 1797), a
ballad by Friedrich Schiller.

this earth".* The street feuilletonist, as graceful as a butter-
fly, resists such temptations. It is enough for him to flutter,
to sip, to sample with delight like the educated man who
observes rather than the primitive man who grabs or
seizes. He preserves the pure sheen of his serene, amiable
existence under all circumstances. Never has a true feuilletonist been "won over"; never, ever! Oh let us doff our
hats to this man of honour who has such power and uses it
so modestly!

'The salon feuilletonist, *F. nobilis*, comes from the
family of Beau Brummel. Isolated exemplars are to be
found in Vienna, and so I feel duty bound to include
him here, although his natural habitat is actually Paris or
London. German salons do not yet make it a national *point
d'honneur* to treat German literary figures with the defer-
ence that even French of the highest rank pay their
hommes de lettres. Nevertheless, well-written feuilletons
have now become a respectable art form here in Vienna,
too. "A true German can't stand the French / Yet willingly
drinks their wines"** still holds true in all variations and
keys. The salon feuilletonist, as things stand at the
moment, is therefore more a child of his own imagination

* Quotation from Schiller's poem 'Die Worte des Glaubens' (Words of Faith,
1797).
** Quotation from Goethe's *Faust*, from the famous drinking scene in Auer-
bach's Cellar.

than of circumstance. He knows that, in Paris, every room that doesn't have a bed in it is referred to as a salon, and he adheres strictly to this usage. He certainly takes his tea in salons, where he makes occasional bashful attempts to speak of his aristocratic connections and is very *satisfaited* when he finds a gullible soul who believes in them. Despite this, he never takes open scorn and mockery personally; instead, he imitates the poodle politic that, no longer able to carry the sausages it ran off with, scoffed the lot together with its enemies and pursuers. Nevertheless, the salon feuilletonist seeks constantly to recreate the nimbus that has been destroyed, parading before our eyes elegant toilettes, perfumed handkerchiefs, a full inventory of all the superfluous debris considered *nécessaire* by the French, *par exemple* a complete set of hair combs, beard combs, hair brushes, beard brushes that serve him as content, just as reminiscences from Lelly's Chevalier perspective and Wachenhusen's elegant studies serve him as style.[*] This, my dear sir, is the only species for whom you would be justified in suspecting a lack of material; even so, he uses all the tools of his art to make us forget the natural disadvantages of his habitat. And as people under such

---

[*] The Prussian Baron Friedrich Christian Eugen von Vaerst wrote a *Handbook for Would-be Wastrels* in 1836 under the pseudonym of Chevalier de Lelly, using anecdotes from a stay in Paris. Hans Wachenhusen was a German travel journalist and novelist who combined war reporting with society name-dropping.

circumstances tend to make more rather than less of
an effort, we are, when all is said and done, obliged to
acknowledge that this curious species also entertains us
tolerably well in his particular domain with his particular
expertise.

'A less shadowy, stereotyped creature, the tavern feuilletonist, *F. restauratus*, leads a rough and ready existence.
This species is naturalized in the coffeehouse. You will
never find it there with a newspaper, but always with
cards or a billiards cue in its hand. Loathing for periodical
publications of all kinds is a distinguishing characteristic
of this kind of journalist. The distaste with which they view
all possible contact with the daily papers as contamination,
the cold rage with which they sweep these off tables, chairs
and even the billiard table, the expression on their faces
that clearly shows how far they believe we have strayed
from the true purpose of culture by teaching youth to
"read" at all in the first place instead of instructing them
in "Preferanzeln" or "Karambolieren"*—all of this would
set a very dangerous, suicidal example, if the tavern feuilletonist were not also inspired by a fundamental contempt
for the public in his role as misanthrope, egoist, *homme*

* Dialect terms for a card game (like 'snap' but with three players) and for
billiards. Typically for Vienna, these words are not Germanic in origin; most
Viennese slang comes from French (as in these cases), Slavic, or Yiddish sources.

blasé, in short, Mephistopheles. As a writer, the tavern feuilletonist is always a satirist. His silhouettes, physiognomies, daguerreotypes, or whatever name he uses for his portraits of fellow coffeehouse habitués, are polemics against humanity. Oh Herr von Grammelmaier, as I gather your distinguished name to be! may you never have the misfortune to frequent an establishment which is the regular haunt of a tavern feuilletonist! For then, I fear, you would experience what feuilleton material is and how inexhaustible it is at the cost of your own highly estimable person. None is venerable enough, no reputation sufficiently sacred to escape the wit that, in a series of devilish transformations, can always be relied upon to turn respectability into its opposite. Just think of poor old Louis Philippe, a king who was turned into a pear! And the strangest thing about the whole affair would be that, over many years, you would have no idea of who your tormentor was. For if we expect the tavern feuilletonist to observe, to see, to hear in the same way that other people see and hear, we are hugely mistaken. No, the tavern feuilletonist ignores. The card table, billiards, these are the only objects worthy of his attention and only at the moment when he has to "pass" or else it is his opponent's turn to play, which happens seldom enough, does he throw the rest of the world a distracted, weary look through the cold lens of his eye-glass—a look that seems well below freezing point. And yet it is the scorching gaze of an enraged tiger—used to seize the prey that will fill hundreds of feuilletons with their rose-red blood. Ah, Satan sees all; the gods have conferred on him terrible powers of intuition. At the same time, he can *feel* the coffee-house, he has olfactory and sensory powers of detection as well. He complements this genius with the inspiration of the headwaiter. Headwaiter and tavern feuilletonist maintain a curious relationship that is almost impossible to define.

'It is reminiscent in many ways of the relationship between viceroy and pasha in Egypt or else elderly midwife and young woman in childbed. Here we find the same cordial presumption in the feeling of power, the same benevolent tolerance alongside gentle reminders of natural boundaries that nevertheless dissolve repeatedly of their own accord, the same indestructible secret bond born of necessity with all of the familiarity that this creates, accompanied nevertheless the whole while by the need to maintain outward appearances, by the last remnants of social propriety and distance! It is a shadowy, chimerical relationship, but its spawn is terrifyingly real! Woe to the city in which a seasoned headwaiter and a talented feuilletonist hit it off together! It is an alliance to be feared, one that makes the whole population quake in its boots while serving sweet melanges and flavoursome feuilleton articles day by day! Oh, contradictory world!

'And now, finally, we leave the city behind us all together and still find plenty of material, for we are in hot pursuit of the forest feuilletonist, *F. tenebrosus*, from the family of the melancholy Jacques—see Shakespeare. As the name suggests, the forest feuilletonist is to be found "in the forest's furthest reaches, hidden in the darkest caves".* He is the most intimate friend of newts, frogs, slow worms, and otters; his ways are strewn with mushrooms and toadstools, ferns and moss are wreathed about his brow. He smiles pityingly at the Viennese with their much vaunted appreciation of nature and their amateur attempts to organize trips to the countryside, he explores the Himalayas of the Kahlenberg hills far beyond Liesing with its fried chicken and bock beers. No "Rosa" accompanies him, the forest feuilletonist always walks alone. Seen from a distance, he resembles a candidate for suicide. I once secretly followed a man in the Prater with the altruistic intention of saving his life. His gait, posture, movements, everything about him was so endlessly sad that I was utterly convinced he was taking his last walk, towards some arm of the Danube. The

---

* The opening lines of a popular song about the robber chief Rinaldini and his beloved, Rosa. By Christian Vulpius (1762–1827).

unhappy man often stood still and poked in gloomy self-absorption at a molehill with his stick, then he threw his head back to look up into the clouds, yearningly, like someone who is savouring his last, full breaths of God's good air; from time to time he took a notebook out of his pocket and wrote something down that was obviously his last will and testament, in which he would explain his reasons for wishing to depart this life. At last we arrived at the banks of the dreaded Danube. As the river hoved into view, I quickened my steps, realizing in a flash that there was no reason for either of us to get wet; surely I could save him while he was still on land by involving him in a conversation that would take his mind off his unhappy thoughts. I acted immediately. I rushed to his side and wanted to begin right away. However, I was stopped in my tracks by a row of fishermen sitting stiff and immobile on the bank, in the silent attitude typical of their occupation. My suicide candidate went from one to the next and walked around each of them, observing them with minute attention. Using his handkerchief, he made waving movements towards them like someone wiping away dust, causing them to lift their heads and look at him in wonderment. At that, the suicide apologized in very engaging terms, saying that he was unfortunate enough to suffer from severe myopia and had thought that he could see inscriptions on them, for he had taken them to be Roman milestones, possible clues to old Vindobona or Fabiana* that appear out of the Danube when the water levels are low. The following day I read this amusing anecdote alongside many others in one of our best feuilletons; I made a note of the initials under it and found in many, many subsequent issues the most charming still-life descriptions of the Prater, the Prater stags, the fishermen, the beetles and ants, the grasses and trees, the clouds and winds—observed with a fine eye and a genial, inexhaustible humour. These are the standard fare of this feuilletonist: the forest feuilletonist.

'One last hunting ground is worthy of note, a territory that even at first glance seems sure to yield bountiful prey. It is monopolized by the social feuilletonist, *F. aequivocus*. The species of the social feuilletonist is only to be found in the more distant suburbs, in particular in the evenings, at the water fountains and gates of the big factories in Gumpendorf, Schottenfeld, and so on. Here he studies his sources: servants and factory girls, from whom he collects notes about service and employment, supply and demand, salaries, ways of life, in short, about all the small and yet vital details of industrial and proletarian conditions. A considerable undertaking! But the social feuilletonist

---

* Names of the Roman settlements that stood on the site of today's Vienna.

applies himself to his task with great dedication and has a natural talent for dealing with the common people. Unfortunately, the extent of his thirst for knowledge is far too great to be slaked at the small hollow of opportunity to be found between the day, when the girls are at work, and the night, when they are expected home. I freely admit that in the case of this species of feuilletonist, it is not always entirely clear where the boundaries run between the strictly professional and the purely private, the service of public interest and personal sporting interests; as such, a rigorously literary characterization of this species cannot be established with total scientific certainty. But it is enough if I have been able, in these rough outlines, to present you with some of the columns which uphold the entertainment of our city by means of the feuilleton—just a few of them, nothing like the whole colonnade. Imagination and reflection must supply the rest. We've finished eating now, my dear sirs, so with your gracious permission, I'll take my leave.'

With these words, I let the steward help me into my overcoat, which I had been able to do without in April but now find myself needing again in late June. Behind me, a half-audible whisper: I'd say he must surely be a feuilletonist himself . . .

Spas Sleeps

Dimitré Dinev

They found him under a poster. 'Live and Work in Vienna' the poster said. He had done both, now he lay peacefully beneath it. He lay on his back. As the dead hold lit candles placed in their hands—obediently, but diffidently—he held half a can of beer on his belly. But the man was not dead. After all, the poster didn't say 'Work and Die in Vienna'. The man lying on the ground was alive. He was only sleeping and as he wasn't talking in his sleep, no-one could tell that he was a foreigner. His name was Spas Christov. If they had looked in the inside pocket of his winter jacket, they would have found an expired student ID card with the same name on it. The name was genuine. The student card was also genuine, just out of date.

Spas Christov had nothing wrong with him on this cold January evening of the year 2001. He was thirty-six years old, but he looked older in his sleep because he was dreaming, and in his dreams he experienced things that would either never happen or else only happen later. He didn't talk in his sleep, but every now and again his lips moved. If anyone had watched his face for a while, they would have seen that these lips formed one and the same word, over and over again, at irregular intervals. They formed the word so clearly that any passerby would easily have been able to understand it. All they would have had to do was stay a while and take a good look at Spas's face and they would have recognized the word. But no-one stopped to look. And so the word remained unrecognized, just as it had remained unheard. 'Work' was the word that gave Spas's lips no peace. It kept trying to force its way up to the surface, out of his dreams. But no matter how much it tried, it failed to become reality. Spas dreamt many different dreams this night. One followed another, over and over again. But no matter how often his dreams changed, the word remained the same. To begin with, he dreamt of his seven-year-old daughter. She wore a pale yellow dress with ladybirds on it.

'Father, where were you the whole time?' she asked.

'It didn't take any longer than usual, little one.'

'Yes it did, it took ages. My dolly has got married in the meantime.'

'Who to?'

'Someone who doesn't stay away for so long. Where were you?'

'You know where I was, at work.'

Then his lips moved again. When he was asleep, Spas looked older because he often dreamt about things that would only happen later or not at all. He didn't have a daughter. He didn't have a wife. He didn't even have permission to be here at all.

'What's wrong? What's the matter with you?' asked a young passerby who had just discovered him. 'Can you hear me? Can you speak? Do you understand German?' The passerby saw Spas's lips moving silently, making room for a word.

'Arbeit' was the first word that Spas had learnt in German. It wasn't the word for love or hope, let alone faith. Work—without that, there was nothing but fear. At the beginning there was this word. All the others came after it. It was like that for every refugee. Why should it be any different for Spas? He was a refugee too. He had fled Bulgaria eleven years before, full of love, hope, and faith. He wanted to live in Vienna, to love and be loved. So he came. He knew no-one, no-one was waiting for him. But they already knew that many of his kind would come.

They were ready for him. There were places for such un-
announced visitors. There was the camp in Traiskirchen.[*]
They told him how to get there. Spas was happy. He had
finally arrived somewhere where he was expected. Unfortunately, however, he was not the only one. There were
many already there, and many more followed. All with
the same hope, with the same faith. And all of them wanted
the same things as he did. People are the same, no matter
where they come from or where they are going. They
carried on coming, more than expected. And whenever
the number of visitors expected changes, the law changes
as well. There was no asylum any more. There was only a
six-month residence permit and then deportation. Unless,
that is, you found work. Work was the most important
thing. Everyone was looking for it, not everyone found it.
And anyone who didn't find it had to go back. Work was a
magic word. All the other words were inferior to it. It alone
determined everything. Work was more than a word, it
was salvation.

'I'm looking for work' was the first sentence that Spas
had learnt in German. 'Have you found any work?' 'Have
you heard about any work?' the refugees asked one another

---

[*] Traiskirchen is a small town approximately 20 km south of Vienna, where
the former barracks has been used to house refugees since the founding of the
Second Austrian Republic as a neutral state in 1955.

every day. Spas discovered that, regardless of what they had been before, the refugees now divided up into two groups: the ones that had work and the ones that didn't. You only lent money to those who had already found work. Spas also found out that there was 'black' and 'white' work. Just like bread. Except that everyone preferred white. Everyone dreamt of getting legal work, that was salvation. But even black work was better than nothing. It was a comfort. And so everyone did everything they could to get any kind of work. They heard about American sects who made sure their members got work. And so they had themselves baptized. They didn't hope to find God, but work. They went to the Americans. They got wet. They dripped. They smiled shyly. The congregation was pleased. That was all the miracle of baptism had to offer, but sometimes they were offered work as well, and that was nothing short of a miracle. Some went to get baptized several times over, but still no miracle happened. They just got wet more often. That didn't matter. It was only water. They dried off quickly and carried on looking. It was a truly purifying search.

The official information was that you could only get work if you had a work permit. And you could only get a work permit if you had work. This paradox was the cause of many broken hearts. They became cold and hard. They did themselves damage or damaged others. Now and then teeth were lost. Patience and hope were already long gone. People shivered as though they had just been baptized, but they didn't dry out. They wanted to drink. They reached for a bottle. There were so many on the shelves. Beautifully displayed in beautiful shops. They took one. They would pay later, when they had work. They still had a conscience, but no money. That was what it was like for some, but not for all. Most of them didn't give up so easily. Spas was one of these.

After all, his intention had been to study here. He was twenty-five years old, had been in the middle of his history degree in Bulgaria and wanted to carry on with it. He didn't give up on his plan. Many already had—not he. But it was hard, because he was alone with all his hopes and dreams. You need someone to share them with. You need friends, or at least one friend. Even though the search for work sets people against each other. Spas was lucky. He met someone he used to go to primary school with in the camp yard. His name was Ilija.

They had often fought at school. Ilija had broken two of Spas's fingers, Spas had broken Ilija's nose. Whenever they met, there were scratched faces, bruises, dust in their hair and tears in their eyes. They had caused each other plenty of pain. There was blood between them, childhood blood. They recognized one another and embraced. Ilija had a fifty-schilling note.* Caritas had given it to him to buy a ticket to Traiskirchen. Ilija spoke good English. He could explain things. Now he had fifty schillings as well. They bought two bottles of wine and drank. The red of the wine between them was the red of childhood, of Communism and of the dawn light. There was a lot of red between them. They shared it. Their hearts were warmed, the blood high in their cheeks. Their eyes, red from lack of sleep, looked to the future. They were friends.

Spas was sent to a holding centre for asylum seekers in the mountains. Ilija to a boarding house near Vienna. Spas promised he'd come as quickly as possible. Where Spas was, there was nothing but trees, mountains, meadows, and lots and lots of time. The next village was six kilometres away. It was a good place to spend a holiday. Except that there were no holidaymakers in his boarding house, only four refugees from Rumania.

'No work here. Here just quiet. Too quiet—we worry. Work only in city. Big city big work,' they said to him in German. Otherwise they only spoke Rumanian. They waited. Waiting was easier. You could wait without having to say anything. You could only look for work in German. Spas had already understood that work is more important

---

* The 'Schilling' was Austria's currency before the Euro. According to the 2002 exchange rate when Austria joined the Euro, fifty schillings is equivalent to €4.50.

than a roof over your head for six months. Only those who had work were allowed to stay. Only those who had work had a home. He left the holding centre. He needed a home.

Ilija was waiting for him. They went to Vienna every day to look for work. At night they slept in the same bed and dreamt of finding work. Both of them wanted to study as well. The only things they had brought with them were their high school diplomas.

They applied to become students and were accepted. They registered at the University of Vienna. Spas history, Ilija politics. Then they discovered that students get visas as well. That was a bit of a relief. Others discovered this too. Lots of refugees registered to study. They needed relief as well. Work was still the most important thing. You needed it to carry on studying. Now and then they put up posters, handed out fliers, sold magazines. Temporary jobs in the open air, as unreliable as the weather and lashed by the cold wind from the Danube. Temporary jobs that offered no respite.

There was a connection between where you came from and the work you could get. Spas gradually realized that very few of the Bulgarians and Rumanians he knew had work, but all of the Poles did. Even though the jobs were sometimes illegal, they had work. The Poles helped each other. More than the others. It was better to be a Pole. It was even better to be a Greek, Spas knew that too. As a

Greek he got work straight away, over the phone. But he didn't turn up for the job. He wasn't a Greek. Poles didn't need to pretend to be from somewhere else, they found work as Poles. Being Polish was more than a nationality. Being a Pole was a profession. The black Africans were worst off. Being African was a punishment. Best of all was being Austrian. All the refugees agreed on that, that was why they were here, after all. Being Austrian meant salvation.

Spas and Ilija were Bulgarians and that meant having to search on and on, like many other nationalities. A Bulgarian was nothing but a refugee, one of many and unredeemed like all the rest. Being Bulgarian was nothing special. It meant nothing. Spas and Ilija were friends. And that meant looking for work together. It meant sharing a single bed and food for one person. They were two Bulgarians. Being two Bulgarians meant making do with what one needed. Two Bulgarians were worth as much as one person.

In the beginning they went looking together, and then separately, because they could look in more places at the same time, and when they were separated, they both looked for work for two. They cleared snow, they cleared gardens, they cleared warehouses, and they looked up in awe to those who cleaned the streets. Their orange overalls shone. You could see them from far off, like so many rising suns. Heavenly bodies, following their designated earthly course. They were out of reach. They came from another planet. They were Austrians. Only Austrians were allowed to work as refuse collectors. Work was an enchanted word. At no other time did Spas and Ilija feel this more clearly. The street cleaners were wizards. Gold rings gleamed on their fingers, gold chains round their necks, wound around each other like mysterious snakes, like the guardians of hidden treasure. The street sweepers were sworn alchemists. They knew the secret. They collected rubbish that changed into gold and shone on them. Spas and Ilija yearned to be transformed like these. They stared at them entranced. They were stunningly beautiful, these Austrians, as stunning as an epiphany. Spas and Ilija knew that they had to shine at every kind of work. That was their only chance. Every refugee knew this. They had to fight hard to outshine the others. You fought for rays of hope. 'I can climb up high, right up to the heavens, I can work on scaffolding. But I can also work under the earth, in the water and on the ground. Day or night. Black or white. I'm ready for anything and I learn fast.' These were the rays that every refugee sent out. 'I'm looking for work' was what they said. And the more they could say, the brighter they beamed. Language was important. Spas and Ilija learnt fast. They were friends. They shared everything, even words. They told each other everything. Whatever one of them could do, the other soon learnt. There were enough words to go round. You didn't need to look for them for long. They were everywhere. You just had to reach out and take them. You needed courage, as you always do when meeting the unknown for the first time. Spas and Ilija didn't stop for long to think about whether the words were right or wrong. They were looking for work, for salvation. And the words could help.

Spas and Ilija learnt to say 'yes' straight away when anyone asked if they could do this or that, or if they had already done this or that. They said 'yes' even before they knew what kind of work it was. They didn't think much of subjunctives. In this way, Spas found work that looked as though it would last a while. He asked in a restaurant. He said 'yes'. They gave him a white overall. He smiled. Then they gave him a tall, white hat. His smile became a little strained. Explanations and training took all of thirty minutes. And then the miracle happened. Overnight, Spas became a cook. He fried Schnitzel, chicken, mushrooms, cheese, and chips. He boiled egg dumplings, soup with strips of pancake or liver dumplings, frankfurter sausages and smoked sausages. He roasted meat and made salads. That's how easy Austrian cuisine was! And kind, how kind Vesna the waitress was. She helped him. She was a Serb. Her language was closer to his. He understood her words much better. She was helpful and kind. How consoling and kind, the words that we understand. The reward for Spas's hard work, dedication and courage was fifty schillings an hour. He also received a precious promise from the owner of the restaurant that he would be legally employed one day, one bright day. Spas cooked. The faint light of that far-off day before his eyes and the tangible comfort of work in his pocket. At the same time Ilija, transformed into a foaming mug of beer, wandered up and down Kärtner Strasse. He had been lucky too. Two days after his friend's miracle, he also found work. He had gone to ask at a bar and said 'yes' to everything as well. The only difference was that he understood exactly what he had let himself in for. A beer mug sign with jolly, encouraging words on it was strapped to his back. The foam looked like a fluffy cloud and the bar's address was right on top of it. A straightforward matter. A great deal more transparent than baptismal waters. Ilija was to be jolly and sparkling, to exude good faith and good cheer. He was to make those who had enough to eat feel hungry again and those who had plenty to drink feel thirsty; he was to attract customers. He was to go out into the world, down the grand boulevard whose gleaming shop windows already made everyone greedy. He was supposed to get the world to come to the bar. This mission was to earn him praise and sixty schillings an hour. Ilija took it on. Ilija was a fresh, living advert. He walked up and down Kärtner Strasse as a foaming beer. It was winter. He was cold. Beer is supposed to be cold. He had a bitter taste in his mouth. Beer is supposed to be bitter. His eyes misted over from the wind like beer glasses. He was exactly what he was supposed to be. The world foamed around him. He was at one with the world. He had work.

Unfortunately, just like all miracles, these two were also only of short duration. First Spas lost his job. Not because he was a bad cook, but because his boss had gambling debts and the restaurant folded. Ilija lost his job because another refugee turned up who was prepared to be a message on legs for fifty schillings an hour. Ilija would have been just as prepared. But no-one asked him. No-one asks messages anything. They are either sent or received. Now someone else wandered, buffeted by the waves of people, through Kärtner Strasse. A foaming message. The contents were different, but the message stayed the same. It stayed on the foam. Inside, the invisible faces changed. The world only has eyes for exteriors. It doesn't look inside. It doesn't like to open things up. It's frightened of spectres. Spas and Ilija were only frightened of one thing: of having no work again. Work was a spectre. It hid itself from them and tormented everyone. Only those who found it found peace of mind. Six months should be long enough, the law decreed. After that it persecuted anyone who still haunted the place without work: an exorcist who thought six months was long enough to prove who is a person and who is a ghost. The ideal world wished to remain so. The refugees knew this. They found themselves in an ideal world in which every outsider was put to the test. They had known from the start that they would have to put up a fight. They were only surprised that they still had to fight against so many fears in this ideal world. They had difficulty grasping that they themselves had been changed into fears by the law. They were the fears of the ideal world. But they didn't have the time to understand this. They had to fight against fears and they fought against each other.

Spas and Ilija still had four months left to prove themselves. They got by with very little. They would have been content even with illegal work. After all, they were students and as such they were allowed to stay. That afforded them a little relief. But they still weren't able to relax. They carried on looking. To look for work, you needed money. Even if you didn't find work, you still had to pay. Every telephone call, every tram trip required not only effort but also money. They had plenty of energy left. But their money was gradually coming to an end. They began to look for empty bottles with a deposit on them. Then they were able to make more phone calls. Every bottle was a message. They couldn't go on like this for long though. Very soon the bottles were just as hard to find as work itself. They didn't solve the problem. So they looked for another solution. Ilija heard from a Kurd that Caritas gave money to every refugee who wanted to go back home. Spas heard it from an Indian and they had both already heard it from a Pole. So it must be true. And if not, then so what. Ilija knew the way. The Caritas officials knew people like Ilija. They knew that people in need are wilier than the devil, and tried to tell truth from the lies. Spas and Ilija didn't know the devil and of all the possible truths, they only wanted to know one: whether Caritas really gave people money for the journey back home. That was all they hoped for. Their manner was quiet and humble. Their German still wasn't very convincing. So Ilija spoke English. Spas just said 'yes' from time to time. Sometimes twice in quick succession. As he felt necessary. Caritas believed that they wanted to go back home and gave them money, which they then used to carry on looking for work. They received money for the journey and they really did travel. Only they travelled through the city instead of going home. But they travelled. They were believable because they had not lied. For a refugee, work and home were the same. Spas and Ilija were very pleased with the money. They loved all Kurds, Indians, and Poles. They loved Caritas. They loved the world. They didn't need much to love. Less than one person.

When this money ran out as well, they began to give blood. They gave their blood to save strangers' lives and received money that saved their lives. Just like people, the blood was divided up into groups as well. Except that every blood group was worth just as much as all the rest. Anyone could give blood. You didn't need permission. Blood was always needed, sometimes very urgently. More urgently than any permit, than any authorization. It was enough that the blood was pure and good. Spas and Ilija had blood. It was pure and good. They gave of it. Lying next to each other they looked at the red glass containers. They saw the blood of their childhood. They didn't need to break each others' noses anymore to see it. They were as dizzy as babes in a cradle. They got sweets, they got drinks, they were treated well. They laughed like children. They got money. With the payment for the blood of their childhood they carried on searching for a refuge. They carried on searching because you can't live from blood and memories alone. No-one has that much blood, no memory is that sustaining. Work was their aim. A long-term job was worth more than blood and memory.

Then Spas and Ilija heard of a place where instead of searching all you had to do was wait. People told them it was in Herbststrasse, opposite the job centre. That was where they should go. Workers' strip, it was called, another Bulgarian told them. They went. Opposite the job centre stood a long row of people. Men of all nations. Spas and Ilija joined them. Cars drove past slowly. Sometimes they stopped and took someone from the row with them. They were important cars. The people who sat inside picked and chose and showed mercy. There was not a lot of this to go round but some days, there was even enough for Spas and Ilija. Then they renovated apartments or built houses. The days were long, their hands covered in calluses, their fingernails broken. Only then were they allowed to get their hands on the money they longed for. 'Know what, boys,' the foreman once said to them. There was always a foreman. This one was a Croat. 'Know what,' he said after work, 'yesterday I am together with girlfriend. I love she very much. Yesterday even more. I want stroke her thigh. Wait, wait, she say. You ruin my tights. Your hands is sandpaper.' He laughed. Spas and Ilija laughed too. They had no girlfriend, but they had hands that would be the ruin of any nylons in the world.

Unfortunately these jobs could not be relied on. The workers' strip wasn't safe either. Policemen came and asked what they were doing there. Everyone knew to say that they were waiting for a friend. Which, after all, was surely true? The policemen smiled and came in plain clothes. They came as friends. They sat in cars and offered work. Some got in. When they arrived there was in fact plenty for them to do. Spas and Ilija were warned by an Albanian who had already been on this unhappy journey. They thanked him and left the strip. Everything was as it had been before. Except that there was even less time left. And a little less hope. And a little less faith. But they didn't need much. It was enough if one of them still hoped, if one of them still looked. It didn't matter which one. And one day it came to pass that they really did find work. Illegal work, but long-term. As ever, they had said 'yes' and were given a job as waiters in a bar.

Their shift ended sometime between 2 and 3am. They couldn't get back to the home for asylum seekers at that time of the morning. It had been hard enough to find work, but it was even harder to hold on to it. Both of them knew that very well. You can live without a roof over your head, but not without work. So they slept on the streets. They lay down in parks, hidden in the bushes and tried to sleep. It was still far too cold. A homeless man told them they should look for big containers. They were cosy, dry, and full of sand. In case of snow. He was right. The containers were cosy. Spas and Ilija slept there and went to work as waiters afterwards. One night it snowed. Someone came looking for sand and found Spas and Ilija. He wasn't scared. He knew all about snow, sand, and people. He was Russian, a refugee called Mischa. Spas and Ilija could speak Russian. 'I know something better,' Mischa said. They followed him. He led them to a depot and kissed the bearded security guard three times. After that, the security guard hugged Spas and Ilija. His name was Georgi. He couldn't bear solitude and had a warm heart. Just like the hearts of all Georgians. In the yard of the depot, Mischa showed them a train. Five old carriages that had once travelled the world. They still stuck together closely, even closer now because of the rust, but they didn't travel any more. This train was going nowhere. All three got in. There were people sleeping in almost every compartment. Mischa led them to their compartment. There was no need to pay a fare. All you had to do was to hug the security guard from time to time, Mischa said, and went to sleep in the compartment next door. Every morning people got out of the train and went to work. A train that wasn't going anywhere took them to their work. Soon Spas and Ilija got to know other passengers. Spas liked the Rumanian Jakob and his six-year-old daughter Anka best. She always wore a pale yellow skirt with ladybirds on it and played the recorder. Spas liked Anka best of all. He often wished he had a daughter just like her. He wanted a wife too but a daughter even more. He saw Anka once playing in an underground metro station. He gave her money, but she didn't recognize him. While she was playing, she only recognized the people she was playing for. She hadn't been playing for Spas. When he saw her, she had been playing for her mother, and she lived a long, long way away, she explained to him later in the train. Spas often brought her sweets, and once he even bought her a little doll. Everyone brought her things, everyone loved her. She was the only woman among them. All of them gave her the love that they missed.

The funniest of all were the Nigerian Sunday and Samuel from Ghana. 'Sunday, are there crocodiles in Nigeria?' Ilija asked him once. It was night. Ilija and Spas had an evening off. It was too cold to sleep and they were sitting together with Sunday and Samuel in one of the compartments. A bottle of schnaps changed hands in the darkness, it was like a long and entertaining journey. 'Many, many crocodiles in Nigeria, crocodiles always very, very hungry. They look for food. Man must be careful. Man thinks much of himself, but for crocodile still just food,' Sunday began and took a gulp. 'But in a village I saw very many. One over the other, in a pond. There they are holy. They are hungry like the rest, but holy. They not look for food. Man gives them food. I see. Man throw it from far away. They jump over each other and all food gone quickly. Some stay hungry, of course, because so many are holy.' Sunday laughed. He had been condemned to death in Nigeria and only had a month left to find work. Sunday laughed. He was hungry too. He was one holy crocodile too many. Everyone laughed. It was cold in the train. You couldn't sleep, but you could laugh.

Spas and Ilija were good waiters. They always worked together. Their German wasn't good enough yet and it was difficult. But whenever one of them didn't understand a word, he asked the other. When neither of them understood—for often people ordered things that weren't on the menu or in the dictionary—then logic, imagination and intuition were called for. At the beginning they were afraid of asking anyone else what a word meant, for they didn't want to give the impression that they couldn't speak the language well or that they were bad waiters. They wanted to keep their jobs. Spas and Ilija were friends. They shared everything. Even the words they didn't understand. And because there were still plenty of these, they learned to guess what it was that people wanted. Spas and Ilija were good waiters. They got lots of tips, because they were able to guess their customers' wishes even before they had spoken them aloud.

But Spas and Ilija didn't just want to work, they wanted to study as well. They hadn't forgotten the dream they shared. Before starting university, they had to pass a German exam. You learnt lots in a bar, but unfortunately, the German that you learnt there was not enough to pass an exam. They paid for an intensive German course. The money that they got every time they guessed what someone wanted was now spent on learning the many incomprehensible words that made up all those wishes. They had to demonstrate knowledge and not intuition. Grammar and rules were examined, not supernatural abilities. For it was the law that examined, it was people, and not spirits. Spas and Ilija learned German, waited tables and did their homework in one of the train compartments. Sometimes the other passengers helped them. 'Where do you come from?' the textbook asked. 'From necessity,' Jakob said. 'What are your parents' names?' 'Write poverty and hunger,' Sunday suggested. 'But my mother's name is Irina,' Anka said sadly. 'Your mother's different. Write her name on the window with your finger. You can look out through the letters then. Only your mother has letters like that,' Sunday reassured her. 'Where do you live?' was the next question in the book. 'In a luxury private express train,' Mischa threw in. 'Where are you going?' 'Right on by, past the big money,' Georgi sang. It was fun doing homework together. They didn't have a home, but they had work. That was entertainment enough.

Spas and Ilija passed the exam first time. They sat in the same room, one behind the other. What one didn't know, the other did. When they got back to the yard in the depot, they found everyone standing in front of the train. Mischa and Georgi, the security guard, both drunk, were trying to pull the train. All the others were laughing or egging them on. 'Please, please don't,' shouted Anka, 'otherwise we won't have anywhere to live!' These words went straight to Georgi's heart, and he had a big heart. He straightened up. 'Pack it in, Mischa, stop messing around!' he ordered. 'And by the way, I love you all, and don't want you to leave,' he said as well, and hugged everyone with the same strength that he had pulled the train with. Not Anka. He lifted Anka up, high into the air above all the others, and told her to try the Milky Way and see what it tasted like. There was no milk up there in the sky, she replied. 'Well, then, let's drink vodka instead,' he said, and put her down again. Then everyone discovered that Spas and Ilija had passed the exam. That called for a celebration. They had both brought something with them. Everyone got into the train again and with every glass of vodka they passed another station. They didn't care where they were going. Only Anka looked through the window and was sorry that the sky wouldn't come any closer so that she could taste its milk.

Mischa had told Spas and Ilija to save up five thousand schillings for an apartment he knew that they could get without a deposit. When they'd finally got the money together, he took them there. It was a house where only Russian Jews lived. Refugees waiting to leave for America. They asked Spas and Ilija if they were Jews too. Spas automatically answered 'yes'. They would have got the apartment anyway, but Spas said that he was a Jew. He would also have liked to be a Pole and a Greek and in particular an Austrian, so why not a Jew as well. He had often not been given work because people thought he came from Turkey or Yugoslavia. And when he said he came from Bulgaria he didn't get any because they suddenly decided he must be a Jew. Jews could come from anywhere. To be a Jew, you only need black or reddish hair and a long nose. Spas had black hair and a long nose. He wasn't actually a Jew, but he had as much right as anyone in this world to call himself one. They got the apartment. It was a one-room apartment with a shower and a little kitchen. Finally, they could start studying. They saved money as well, because they were working illegally and you never knew how long such work would last. And when the six months were over, they were able to show the police proof of address, a social security number, proof of matriculation and the bankbook from their savings account. As ever, both of them showed the same bankbook. That was enough. And they stayed in Austria. But the laws kept changing because more and more people came. Lots from Bosnia. The six-month deadline didn't exist anymore. The law shortened and limited everything. Places, spaces, deadlines, and above all movement.

It pushed everyone closer to the border all the time. Later, refugees were stopped at the border straight away and their fate decided in three days. The law knew nothing but borders because it was one itself. The new refugees were changed into fears even more quickly. And refugees arrived who were never ill because they had no health insurance. They worked fast and well, without making any mistakes, because they had no time to learn the language and could only speak through their deeds. They hardly ate, drank, or slept any more, they hardly even breathed, because ten of them lived in twenty-square-metre flats. They had no bodies and were as soundless as shadows. The law persecuted them, but managed to lay hold of fewer and fewer of them, for it had been made for people and not for shadows.

In places where borders keep changing, time passes quickly. After a couple of months, when Spas and Ilija wanted to visit their friends in the train again, there was a new security guard. He drank as well, and although he didn't have a full beard, he did have a moustache. But his heart was not as big as Georgi's. It could stand the solitude just as well as a nutshell can withstand the pressure of powerless hands. They could get nothing out of him. He knew nothing about the train. They went away despondently. They had missed their connection after all.

A year later, they met Mischa by chance. He was driving a taxi. He told them he always had a roof over his head now and that he was saving up to go to South Africa. And the others? He wasn't sure about all of them. Anka had been lucky. Her father had found someone to adopt her. That way, at least she could stay here even though he couldn't. Sunday and Samuel had headed off to Holland. He didn't know whether they had made it or not. He wasn't worried about Georgi. He had had a work permit after all. Mischa promised to visit them, but never came. Perhaps he'd decided to have a look round South Africa first after all. The years passed quickly. They passed in fear of losing their jobs and the effort of keeping up their studies. Spas and Ilija also had to take a Latin exam. They managed that one as well. But they only made very slow progress at university. It wasn't possible to study any quicker because they were full of fear and had to work hard. Work was more important. It was still the decisive thing. Spas and Ilija didn't have much time. The sum of money the police needed to see in their bankbook got bigger year by year. So they saved. They got by with very little, but to study, even if you don't need anything else, you at least need time. After five years they still didn't really have much to show for their time at university. They couldn't go on like this, for they shared the same dream. Sharing the same failure wasn't an option. Success was still possible, much more possible than the fulfilment of an individual dream. And there was no need for a friend if all you were going to do was fail. Both of them felt, both thought the same thing. Ilija was the one who said it aloud: 'Let's do it like this. One of us works, the other studies. The one who studies will be finished quicker. Perhaps it will be easier for him to get a proper job then. If not, then he can carry on working illegally until the other has finished studying.'

'Agreed, but who decides?'

'Fate,' said Ilija and pointed to a dice.

'Whoever throws the highest number two times out of three gets to study.'

They threw the dice. Ilija got to study. They had shared everything. After this fateful decision both of them kept their feelings to themselves, however. Spas obeyed, but it hurt. They made do with little, but it hurt a lot. And this pain could not be shared. It belonged to Spas alone. Ilija felt this, and did everything he could to lessen the pain. He knew that his friend had little opportunity to go out and enjoy himself, so he didn't go out either. Spas couldn't have a girlfriend, so Ilija shared his solitude. Wherever and whatever he could share, he did. It all went well for a year. After that, Spas lost his job. The laws had become very strict. The police inspected bars and restaurants more and more often. His boss got frightened and fired all his illegal workers. Spas and Ilija had to start all over again. They had to look for work together. One time, one of them found work, another time, the other. Little jobs that helped neither one of them. They also had to carry on taking exams, because you couldn't get a visa without passing a certain number of exams. Another year passed. The word work on their lips and before their eyes the whole time. It lay heavy on their hearts, it weighed on their souls and dreams. Once again, it was a spectre that haunted them. Their savings melted away. The border moved closer and closer. Many Russian Jews lived in their house, waiting to go to Australia or Canada, but most of them waiting to go to America. Now and then, some of them brought Spas and Ilija something to eat, some of them lent them money and, out of sheer happiness, forgot to ask for it back on the day they left. However, most of them were poor and had to be careful of every penny themselves, as they didn't know how long they would have to wait. Sometimes it took a year, sometimes longer. Depending on what fate had in store for them. Fate may have been miserly with every-thing else, but it was generous with time. So Spas and Ilija shared their discontent and complained together with them about the ways of the world in general and the ways of the owner of the house in particular, who asked for higher and higher rents and made the most of their helplessness. After such evenings they all went to bed, not any more satisfied than before, but relieved nevertheless and their sleep was deep and good. But Nadeschda Osipovna was the one who helped them most of all. She was a professor of literature and was waiting with her two small children for an American visa. Her husband was already there and sent her long, moving letters full of self-pity that trembled silently in her hands. The trembling carried over to Nadja's lips. Spas and Ilija loved to visit her. She was a wonderful cook and spoke even more wonderfully about Russian literature. Only when they were with her did they manage, for a little while at least, to liberate themselves from the spectre of work. When she recited poetry or spoke about literature, her love for it exalted her so much that it was easy for Spas and Ilija to borrow money from her afterwards. To thank her, they sometimes helped clean her flat, they helped rearrange the furniture, they mended doors and drawers and repaired electric appliances. They went shopping for her or else took her letters to the post office. She didn't need very much help though, much less than all they would have liked to give her. They owed her most of all. Money included. When the day of her departure came, they asked for her address, so that they could at least send her the money in the post. 'Here it is,' said Nadja, and gave them an envelope. Then she hugged both of them and got into a taxi with her children. Shaken by their loss, they forgot about the envelope and didn't open it until later in their room. They found 500 schillings and a note. The note said: 'To dear uncle in the big city'. Nadja loved literature, and she loved Chekhov best of all.

Fate decreed that Spas find work as a carpenter. He had learned to work with wood at school. Although he had attended a grammar school, the Communist regime had wanted every grammar school pupil to prepare for a life of work as well. This Communist ideal now came in useful. He began to work as a carpenter and it looked as though he might be able to stay there. 'Shall I carry on looking for work, or shall I study?' Ilija asked him. 'Study,' said Spas, although he wanted to say another word. But he hated the other word far too much to want to propose it to his friend. Ilija studied. Spas sawed, planed, sanded. Ilija was studying very slowly, Spas thought, and tried to avoid him as much as possible. Spas's job meant that he had to give up his place at university, and so he was no longer able to extend his visa. The visa ran out, he stayed. He no longer knew what he was hoping for. He worked together with a fifty-year-old Czech by the name of Pavel. Pavel slept in the workshop during the week and went home at the weekends. Czechs didn't need visas. Spas thought that perhaps some day, Bulgarians wouldn't need visas either. He didn't hope for it, he just thought it. He seldom spoke to Ilija. Sometimes they drank a bottle of wine together. There was red between them, but it wasn't red enough any more. Spas would have preferred to bash in Ilija's nose again to see the blood of their childhood. But he didn't do it. They had no childhood any more. They had blood-red eyes from lack of sleep. They didn't talk. They had shared everything, now they even shared their silence. The years passed. Spas brought home the money and kept out of Ilija's way. Ilija understood this and said nothing. He had too great a respect for work. They lived together in one flat, but were as distant from each other as different planets. It could have gone on like this forever. But today, Spas's boss had told him that someone had reported the workshop to the police and that he would have to close it for a while, he didn't know how long. First Spas and Pavel drank a bottle of Fernet together. Then Spas accompanied Pavel to Wien Mitte station, where he took his bus to Brno. 'Look,' said Pavel, 'buses are always arriving here. This is where the Czechs arrive in Austria. They travel, but they carry tools in their suitcases. People don't travel to see the world any more. They come here to work, to repair things. Is that normal? It's out of order. The world is broken. That's why they all have to travel with a tool kit.' Pavel left. Spas stayed. He watched the buses coming and going. He didn't want to go home. At Wien Mitte, where so many people came and went, he met Johann, a homeless man. He was always there. You could carry on drinking with him then and there. 'Drinking is dangerous, smoking is dangerous, the doctors say. But none of that shitty lot tell you that working is dangerous,' Johann said and pointed to his mutilated hand. 'After I had that accident at work, no one wanted to give me another job. Now they say I'm dangerous. It's a shitty life,' Johann finished his story and took a gulp. Spas agreed with him. But at some point he couldn't carry on drinking. He went, but his legs were only of use to him for a short while. They let him down in front of a poster that said 'Live and Work in Vienna'. Spas sank to the ground and fell asleep. Johann carried on talking loudly for a while, but soon his throat was too dry and he set off to do something about this dryness. That was when he noticed the man lying beneath the poster. For Johann it was the most natural thing in the world for people to simply lie down where they were. The man had a beer. That wasn't exactly great, but at the moment it would do for Johann. He took the beer and went on his way. Spas continued to lie there. Some saw him, some didn't. Some pretended they hadn't seen him. It took a while until a young passerby discovered him and bent over him. He understood the movement of Spas's lips as signs of life and phoned for help. First an ambulance will come, closely followed by the police. The paramedics will put on their rubber gloves and carry Spas away. In the hospital, they will find out that Spas is not insured. The police will discover that his visa has expired. He will be deported, and he won't hold it against them, because they are only doing their job. Just like in every country where there is law and order. That was what Spas expected as he slept and dreamt that he met his grown-up daughter, who was sticking posters on a wall.

'What are you doing here?' he asked her.

'Can't you see? I'm working, father.'

'You're taller than I am now.'

'Yes I am.'

'How quickly the time passes,' he said and carried on dreaming that he was being deported because he had no work permit. And this is what would happen, as he often dreams of things that are yet to happen. This is what should have happened, but it will not happen. For although Austria is a land of law and order, plenty of unfathomable things still happen here.

They will find him and take him to hospital, that much is certain. But then, after he has slept it off and given them the name and insurance number of his friend, they will let him go home. Spas didn't know that yet. The same way that he didn't know yet that his friend would be waiting at home for him with two bottles of wine. 'I've found legal work. Now I can be your guarantor,' he will say to him. They will sit down together and drink. Their hearts will grow warmer, wider. Finally liberated from the spectre of work, from the terrors of this first word that knocks the breath out of all the others. And there will be many words again, too many to find the right one. 'The love that we missed so much, was it not here between us all the time?' one of them will want to say to the other. But neither of them will. They had shared their words too often, they had used so few of them, and then, when there will suddenly be too many of them, they will stand there helplessly like refugees. They will stand there as they did at the beginning. They will not say the sentence out loud, but they'll both guess it, just as they guessed what their customers wanted to eat and drink. They will just sit there, smiling and drinking, and they will both know what the other is thinking. It will be red and joyful and peaceful, like a meeting of spirits.

That is what will really happen, but Spas didn't know that yet. He slept, and one word moved his mouth. His dreams changed, the word remained. Spas had lived and worked in Vienna for eleven years. Now he was tired, for nothing is as tiring as searching for work, not even the search for meaning. The years had passed by so quickly. As quickly as a dream. And what was he left with? A couple of words that moved his mouth as much when he was awake as when he slept. Words as alive as his lips and as weightless as shadows. But it is only because they are so light that they manage to move from one life to the next. They may remain disregarded, unfulfilled and unheard, but they remain. And even if it is only as a trembling of the lips. And even if it is only as an aftertaste. And even if it is only as this final aftertaste of earth in their roots. They remain. In this mouth and that. The miracles of reality are unheard of.

The Spring Ship

Joseph Roth

Perhaps a light sleeper whose window opens onto the canal heard the panting, rhythmic breaths of the ship's tireless lungs in the night and the soft rattling of chains cast onto the dock as it landed. We'll never know. But in the morning we see that a white steam ship has suddenly appeared. It rubs its cheek against the bank, wraps long clinging chain arms round the posts sticking out of the undergrowth and sinks its sharp iron claws into the soft earth at the water's edge.

On the edge of town, on the banks of the Danube Canal.

It's a spring ship and must surely—who knows?—have surfaced overnight out of depths that were frozen over until now. There's a house on top with innumerable tiny windowpanes, as white as the underside of a leaf. It smokes little blue clouds out of a long, chimney cigar. Ropes and rolls and strange poles, cogs and mysterious gear of all kinds can be seen on deck. On taut lines, nappies and children's clothes blow like sails. Curling waves of silver foam plash around the keel and bows.

The boatman lives on board in a guard's house with his family. It is impossible to say how old he is, and he has stepped straight out of a Theodor Storm novella. The winds of the North Sea are caught in his beard and the smell of salted herring clings to his hands. Naturally, he smokes a short wooden pipe which hangs in the right-hand corner of his mouth like a hooked question mark. He chops wood with slow movements. His wife watches, a baby in her arms.

Children are born here, grow up and turn into old boatmen smelling of salted herring with whiskers and wooden pipes. Whole generations of sailors come and go. I'm sure that their dead are not buried in the Zentral-friedhof,* but wrapped in white sails and lowered on anchor ropes into the deeps, where scaly-tailed nixies take them up in their cool, silvery arms.

---

* Vienna's monumental Central Cemetery, set in stupendous parkland on the eastern edge of the city. A popular Viennese saying describes it as 'half the size of Zurich and twice as much fun'.

When I ask, it turns out that the boatman comes from Neutitschein[*] and works for the Danube Steam Ship Company. He is a very ordinary citizen, knows nothing but the Danube and has never been to the North Sea. He buys his herrings at the delicatessen.

I should never have asked.

Children play on the banks of the Danube Canal. They run back and forwards over the narrow, rocking jetty that sticks out from ship to land like a wooden tongue, and all the while the boatman shouts and threatens. If you listen closely enough, you can hear his Bohemian twang. I should never have listened. I think he's shouting something like: 'gerroff me gangplank!' Or something.

The neighbourhood's washing is spread on the old stones of the bank, which are carpeted with blue-green moss and between which velvety green shocks of grass shoot up, staring the clouds straight in the eye. The houses on the bank of the canal have their windows wide open. Everything offers itself up to the sun.

It is the ship though, glowing and proud, that dominates river and land, houses and people. In the evening, home-comers from the factory put rickety chairs outside their doors, sit in groups and talk about the ship. At night,

[*] Now Novy Jicin in Moravia, Czech Republic.

all the children dream of floating white houses and cursing boatmen, the little girls of sailors and flying Dutchmen.

But one night it disappears again as suddenly as it came.

And I don't believe for a moment that the old boatman has simply moored a few kilometres further downstream, but rather that he is now floating around in his white house on heaven knows what far-off ocean, appearing suddenly as if from nowhere on foreign shores. Perhaps a light sleeper, whose window opens onto the shore, will hear the panting, rhythmic breaths of the ship's tireless lungs in the night and the soft rattling of chains cast as it lands. But we'll never know for certain.

The Prater

Adalbert Stifter

There can be few capital cities in the world that can boast such a thing as our Prater. Is it a park? No. Is it a meadow? No. Is it a garden? No. A wood? No. A fairground? No.— Well, what then? All of these at once. In the east of the city of Vienna, a sizeable island is to be found in the Danube; originally made up of floodplain meadows like so many islands in the Danube where the river flows through low-land, over time it has become a delightful blend of meadow and woodland, park and playground, of teeming prome-nades and the stillest seclusion, raucous beer gardens and peaceful glades.—There must be many Viennese who do not know the charms and attractions of their own Prater, no matter how often they have visited it; for however overwhelming the crush may be in some parts, especially at particular times, other parts are as secluded and lonely as the greatest wilderness, so that when you pace through these meadows and copses, you expect to arrive at a neat little farmhouse rather than the gigantic imperial residence of a great monarchy—but gigantic residences require enormous gardens in which their subjects can disport themselves while still retaining sufficient empty spots for solitary wanderers and observers—and fortunate are we to have the Prater. The Viennese know this very well, and even though at times they only grudgingly admit it, for instance in the hot summer months, they are all the more effusively fond of their Prater at other times, for instance in spring, when it is *bon ton* on particular days to drive in the Prater, or else, for those who cannot afford it, at least to walk there. The first and second days in May are such occasions, also Easter Monday and Whitsuntide. Imagine one of these Prater days now, dear distant reader; follow me there in spirit, and let me set out in these pages what we see.

Over Ferdinandbrücke we go into the purlieu Leopoldstadt, turning right straight away into Jägerzeile, which leads to the Prater; the whole of that fine, uncommonly broad prospect is covered with a black mass of people, in waves so dense that, even if you were bet a duchy to traverse the avenue without brushing against anyone, you perforce would lose your wager. Carriages drive through the midst of this crowd like ships in pack-ice, mostly slowly, often held up and forced to stand still for many minutes at a time, but then, when gaps present themselves, flying past each other like gleaming phantoms through the stolid, meandering mass. Figures on horseback can be seen rearing up out of the sea of pedestrians here and there, hopping over and through the line of carriages; and houses rise calmly up out of the teeming crowd on both sides of the avenue, magnificent edifices for the most part, their windows and balconies occupied by innumerable spectators who watch the gleaming river pass beneath them, feasting their eyes on its lustrous splendour, its finery and frills. Most of the spectators are ladies clad in all the colours of the rainbow, hanging over this spring parade for all the world like the branches of blossom trees. You would think that the population of the entire city suddenly went mad at quarter past four and, in the throes of an *idée fixe*, was now wandering up and down the selfsame street, and you and I, dear stranger, wander with them. Over there, at the end of the street, we can already see the tall trees of the Prater beckoning through the dust; everyone strives towards them as though they held the promise of eternal salvation. Finally we reach the end of long Jägerzeile, the streets fan out in a star-shape and the crowd disperses. Small flags on long poles point in various directions; the one on our left bears the name 'Ferdinands-Nordbahn' on its fluttering tongue, high in the air; and indeed, carriages packed with people fly in the direction of the station building to our left, where fiery steeds stand, whistling and blowing, ready to bear an endless row of wagons out into the Marches[*] or even as far as Brno, which, thanks to these swift steeds, has become one of our suburbs.—The flag in the middle points the way to the swimming baths, which celebrate their seasonal opening once again today; the third bears a name like 'Nador' or 'Sophie' or some such, and a mighty arm indicates the road to the steam ships; in a clearing further to the right we see the wooden huts of the menagerie: gigantic canvases hanging outside bear depictions that are even more terrible to behold than the monstrous beasts within. These pictures and the exotic calls, whistles, clucks, and roars to be heard from the huts attract many people; there is a dense crowd before the entrance and in the shining eyes of children and country girls you can already observe a lively desire to see what on earth might be inside. In this grassy clearing there are also stalls with fruit and baked goods, a Croat with sponges and flints, a man selling walking sticks and another playing a hurdy-gurdy with a dog on top, which—look!—can stand on two legs and shoulder a sword with its paws.—But most of the masses go past all

[*] The 'Marchfeld' region to the east of Vienna, which gets its name from the river March that runs through it, but also from its status as a border area on the edge of the Czech, Slovakian, and Hungarian provinces.

these things into the broad central avenue known as the Hauptallee, for there the highest, high and lowliest of Viennese society are to be seen—whatever whim and wealth are able to conjure up in the way of splendid raiment, carriages, and servants is on display today in the Hauptallee. There are shady tracks to the left and right, one for pedestrians, one for riders; several thousand carriages drive along the central avenue in close succession. For safety's sake, they drive up one side and down the other, and many of them complete this circuit many times, the better to see and be seen—this then is what the people have come for, this is where the eye is stunned by the quick succession of colour, ornament, finery, crowds, and movement, making anyone unused to such a spectacle feel giddy. Spectators stand crammed together on either side of the avenue, and at their backs the gaudy masses stream past, while in the centre carriage after carriage rolls by, a gleaming, shining row that must be over half a mile long. There, a lady of the highest order floats along in her carriage, moving as lightly as an airship; she is dressed with splendid simplicity, her jewels are few yet precious; right behind her, the family of a rich burgher, followed by a carriage full of merry children, whose astonishment and delight at the splendour surrounding them knows no bounds, and then a man all alone in his carriage and parading for the first time with four incomparable horses;

here riders spring past and offer greetings to a carriage out of which the most beautiful of faces nods back, there a lonely old man sits in his heavy coach, dressed in fine black cloth and bearing many tiny crosses on his breast; he is followed by a hansom cab full of jubilant shop-boys or students—and then another and yet another, the parade dances before your eyes as though it would never stop and finery and splendour bring forth finery and splendour in an unending stream, and as it wells and springs and flows, you are nevertheless witness to a scene which only the Prater can offer: a stag stands very close to the festive crowds, head with the magnificent antlers thrown back, staring into the fray with dumb yet cunning eyes; it has seen all of this often enough before, but the scene was never as frenetic as today; that's why it stands and stares for several moments before turning aside again, back into its forest glades; for their part, the crowd is not particularly surprised to see the stag either, for they know that the Prater is there for grazing deer as well as promenading pleasure-seekers. And the row of carriages flows on and on—but no matter how magnificent the raiment, how gorgeous the horses and carriages, and no matter how the waving feathers and the dazzling jewels numb your gaze, there emerges from the crowd—more often than you would think—a visage that, as its floats by, makes you forget all else in its gentle beauty. You cannot help but follow it with your eyes and feel poorer when it has passed. Only wait, Vienna is by no means wanting in charming females, perhaps another such will come by presently or else one even more beautiful. Look over there, what is causing that whole line of people to tear off their hats? Six white horses pulling a magnificent carriage.—Who sits within?—The emperor and empress. You're surprised? Something you didn't see in Paris? Here the people wave in greeting and are not at all surprised that they drive here without ceremony, as private citizens among private citizens; the Viennese are used to it and their rulers know that they are as safe in the densest of crowds as in their palace.—But look, the Hero of Aspern is here too;[*] look, just there, that dark-haired man going down the riders' track with another, greeted by all—and only wait, I'm sure we'll see other members of the imperial family on this day of shared pleasures. The carriage with six white horses drives down the avenue into line, just like the hansom cab that wheezes past with two lacklustre duns.

Come now, let us promenade down the avenue, then off to the side to see what the Prater has to offer besides this bewildering flood of faces, clothes and carriages. But the further we venture, the worse it seems to become. The

---

[*] Archduke Karl, Prince of Austria, Bohemia, and Hungary, Generalissimo and Field Marshall of the imperial army, who was the first to defeat Napoleon in battle at Aspern to the east of Vienna in 1809.

knot of people is denser yet calmer. To the left there are places to eat and drink, known as Prater coffee-houses; music sounds from them; many thousands of chairs stand under the trees, overgrown with richly adorned human vegetation—there is conversation, laughter, a roar of voices, tinkling glasses, shouts for waiters—and before our eyes, the gleaming wagons spool on by, up and down the avenue as far as the eye can see, as though it would never come to an end.

More select society disports itself here, whereas further left we see the diversions of the common folk. They are not content with mere strolling or driving, but demand more tangible pleasures and these are spread out here, round about and everywhere. If we leave the current of the Hauptallee by stepping to the left here—a wide grassy clearing with ancient trees awaits us, studded with all that is necessary for the entertainment of the people: there are all sorts of cosmo-, pano- and dioramas; wax sculptures of anything or anyone who was ever famous stand in that hut over there. There is someone on display because he is too big, another because he is too small; one eats fire, another spits skeins of silk, and the chest of a third is subjected to the terrible blows of a hammer like an anvil. Amongst all this, we hear the tapping and jingling of the clown about to begin a new show in his high, narrow stall; over there the dense reddish mob of drinkers clings so closely to the beer stall you would think the poor, beleaguered hut has no room to move in the midst of all those people. One or two are elevated over the masses on a stage, playing scenes that are the object of praise and laughter, on the other side of the tree someone is declaiming verse, and a harpist tears madly at the strings of his instrument to make it and the songs of his companion heard above the fray. Right next to him, harmonium and pipes play in competition; further off, the fainter tones of a hurdy-gurdy can be heard, and glasses are banged on tables and there are shouts and onlookers who wind their way through the mayhem—and if you turn aside, you'll see that over there, under even bigger trees, there is another such beer stall, and to the right another and further off yet another—and everywhere the same tableau is repeated or else an even livelier one—and music resounds through the branches—why it is known as Turkish music is instantly clear—frenzied cavorting from the bass drum and a shimmering and clashing underlying the whole as though a brassmonger had gone mad, and to this cacophony, riders on wooden horses fly around on a carousel, striking the heads off Turks and others. It is not only small boys who delight in this carousel but also apprentices and their sweethearts. She shows herself off in one of the revolving carriages while he runs Turks through—and anyone who's had enough or feels nauseous

gets off and new pleasure-seekers get on and the drum swings with renewed vigour and the carousel spins and through the trees, during the brief moment that they were still, the same music resounded from another such attraction. Over there, whole freights of people are being tossed to and fro on swings until the ropes creak and the trees bend. Others are wound up like pieces of yarn and two lovers get into a fight as she *does* want to go home now and he *doesn't* yet.—As you'll already have guessed from this description, dear unknown reader, you find yourself in the midst of the so-called Wurstlprater, which got its name from the Hans Wurst who is now, however, long dead.*
The splendour and finery in the Hauptallee were already dazzling enough, although they unfurled in a comparatively calm manner before your gaze. Here, however, finery and splendour are the last things you would look for; if you are not used to this element or cannot find a way to countenance it, it will make you take leave of your senses, and I knew an earnest man with weak nerves who held his head in both hands, for he claimed it made him feel as though his skull was being torn apart—but, when all is said

---

* 'Wurst' = sausage, 'Wurstl' = the Austrian diminutive form, also used to denote a laughable figure. 'Hans Wurst' (Johnnie Sausage) is the name of a buffoonish character popular in improvised theatre. Referred to here is almost certainly the Viennese comic Joseph Anton Stranitzky, who made the role his own in the early eighteenth century.

and done, what matter! These are the genuine, hearty pleasures of the common folk, made by the people for the people, and suited to their appetites; let them joke and make merry, even though the jokes are crude: they need the wine of merriment to be strong and rather sour, as its effects have to last through all the humdrum working days to be endured before another feast day like today comes around—that's why the workers look forward to this for weeks in advance, and would not miss it even if they were at death's door—and it is my opinion that, as most of the population of the city is condemned to spend most of their life in airless, cramped workshops in a spirit of airless, cramped narrow-mindedness, the least they should be granted is to open their eyes once in a while, to broaden their horizons and let merriment and pleasure rule—indeed, they should be encouraged so to do. Pettifogging critics may find this merriment and pleasure irresponsible or too coarse, but instead of finding fault, they should be sorry that the plight of common man did not allow him to develop a taste for higher pleasures in his youth.—Do not spoil his fun, o pettifogger, with your refined, sourpuss face; get you gone—or rather, stay where you are, he pays you scant attention in any case. A well-entertained population is an obedient one, as we know full well on the banks of the Danube; and we are glad that this is particularly true in Vienna, where work and pleasure and pleasure and work are mixed in such a way that it is impossible to say which is more important—probably both—you must have heard of the merry folk of the Phaeacians, it's always Sunday here, and 'the roast always turns on the spit'.[*]

Linger here a little longer—Vienna is the city of music, you know—here there is music enough; Turkish tones, the hurdy-gurdy man, the harpist and troubadours, quixotic apprentices with guitars, a pair of maidens belting out a ballad, eternally a fifth apart like two parallel lines—groups of friends returning home with linked arms, singing the deeds of Rinaldo Rinaldini[**]—here and there a young lad with a mouth organ in his hands—and now here come the gypsies as well, strange, stiff fellows; a dream, figures left over from the prehistoric period, untouched by modernity; presently you'll hear how they would remain untouched by the spirit and ways of our music-making even if they were to sit in the Prater their whole life long: the ancient melodies they raise are as fiery and melancholy as their

---

[*] Reference to Goethe's distich on the Viennese in *Xenien*: 'Mich umwohnet mit glänzendem Aug' das Volk der Fajaken, / Immer ist's Sonntag, es dreht immer am Herd sich der Spiess,' [I am surrounded by the people of the Phaeacians with their shining eyes / it's always Sunday, and there's always a roast turning on the spit] which in its turn is a reference to the easy-living Phaeacians who greet Odysseus with great hospitality on the island of Scheria in Homer's *Odyssey*.

[**] A Robin-Hood-like outlaw figure, popularized in ballad form (also referenced in Kürnberger's story 'The Feuilletonists').

eyes, and as fantastically confused and meandering as the strands of their story running through the other stories of world history.—And there is such lamenting and defiance in the drawn-out tones of their violin, soaring ever higher, that I cannot but find it uncanny, every time, yet it never fails to bind and haunt me—this unique, outlandish poetry. And just look at the lead violinist and the cymbal player, one plies his bow and fiddles almost as gracefully as a virtuoso, and look how the other wields his stick, both so earnest and almost sad, turning the whites of their eyes up out of their deep brown faces—and despite the noise and turmoil and music round about, their sound can still be heard—an alien element that calls and sings above all the rest, recognizable from as far away as any music can be heard at all.

Wilder and wilder they play, dashing and plunging with their bows so that the music shoots up like fireworks.—Now the pandemonium is complete, there are more and more people and carriages come by to watch as well; the wine begins to take effect; voices are lifted in raucous song—only two on-lookers remain utterly still and agreeable: the dear evening sun, which pours its light through the reddish dust to bathe all the faces of the crowd, and the delicately budding leaves on the gigantic trees, which sense the balmy spring air and grow and flourish by the hour.

Let us press on and leave this roiling witches' brew behind us so that we can visit other parts of the Prater before the sun goes down. We walk on over grassy glens beneath the enormous trees, and the masses become sparser and sparser and the jumble of music and noise fainter and fainter—occasional groups and couples, also seeking respite from the crowds, enjoy the spring air as they wander happily on grass that is already green. Over there, there's an almighty wooden frame. It's for firework displays, and when the firework artist Stuwer sets light to his fantasies here, instead of the scattered groups we see now, a mass of people stands cheek by jowl as though the place were paved with human heads. Everyone stares up into the night sky as it is cut through by shrieking rockets, or else a star suddenly hangs in the dark heavens, glowing now red, now green, now blue, now golden and, carried by the breeze, drifts slowly down and sidewards,* or else it explodes, throwing a handful of gaudy fire flowers through the night sky—or else a ruined, flaming city suddenly stands before you and, crackling peacefully, gradually burns away, often performing the most expressive romances to the sensitive eye—however, there is none of this today, and the grey scaffolding stands alone in the clearing, peacefully illuminated by the gleam of the spring evening sunshine.

---

* Parachute rockets.

Let's go on until we reach the banks of the Danube. On this dam to the left are the swimming baths, which we'll look at another time; the other wooden houses on pontoons are all bathing and swimming establishments and very busy in the summer months. This is one of the river's wider arms, and over there is what's known as the Freibad, where you can see all those stakes standing in the water: a place cordoned off with ropes for anyone to go for a swim. Let's go further down river here—you see how big our Prater, the garden of Vienna, is—you haven't heard any music for a while now, no more rolling of the thousand or more carriage wheels on the Hauptallee—you have been washed up by the loud, high tide of common merriment, and here on the shore it is already as lonely as in a remote forest glade. Let us walk along the water's edge. A stag grazes on yonder island, and the many tracks on the loamy banks show how often herds of deer ford the river; a herd of cattle stands even further out, at the tip of the thickly overgrown island, and you can almost imagine how the sound of their bells floats over the water—but it is an illusion; the Danube is so wide here that the animals on the other side look like small, brindled lambs. How restorative and gentle are the calm and the soft spring landscape after the turmoil we have just escaped! There is virtually no-one to bother us here; individual fishermen celebrate May Day by standing completely immobile at the water's edge with unfeasibly long rods, but every one of them is an integral part of the landscape rather than a disturbance. Our path takes us ever further down river; that tower glinting in the distance over the water meadows belongs to Ebersdorf, a village that lies more than a mile away from Vienna. Now we are on the shore of the Danube proper; the steamships that travel down river dock just over there, by the mills (known as the emperor's mills) that you can see turning.[*] Further down it gets more and more countrified and deserted. It's strange that you hear so many Viennese complain about life in the city, and say how lovely and invigorating a walk in the countryside can be—but although they have a park full of such charming contrasts closer than any other city, so few come here; and it is the most beautiful parts of the Prater—most beautiful because most natural and unspoilt—that have the fewest visitors. We are walking on narrow paths through the bushes now and arrive at a meadow in a clearing set with splendid, tall trees; crimson rays of evening sun slant through the foliage and branches, and black birds and finches warble their merry song; a rabbit runs through the grass; nowhere is even the tiniest indication of the city to be seen, and we begin to doubt that just a half

---

[*] Now Kaisermühlen, part of Vienna's twenty-second district.

hour before, we found ourselves in the midst of such a teeming, uproarious crowd.—Just look at the elms, and the white poplars—the most common tree to be found on the Danube islands—you would be hard pressed to find these anywhere else in such size and splendour. Here they are spared and none are felled until they die, so that they can spread and develop and flourish in this soft, fertile ground until they reach the limit of their natural life. The Viennese are particularly fond of these beautiful, enormous trees with their broad canopies and I would advise against damaging any tree in the presence of natives strolling by. Standing individually on choice ground, these trees are like precious treasure to the city dweller; the passerby strolls from shade to shade, the pensive, the brooder, the philosopher, the reader prop themselves up against a trunk and immerse themselves in their thoughts or book; the weary worker or the idler doze in their shade; they are joined by the wild fellow who needs to sleep off yesterday's dissolution; the wanderer passes by all of these without disturbing them; the artist sits with his folder on a low stool and draws or paints a tree or group of trees; and there is surely not a portfolio in all of Vienna, whether it be of artist or amateur, that does not contain such 'views of the Prater'. The curious passer-by or lady who makes her carriage wait at one side walk across the grass to stand at the artist's shoulder and peer at his paper to see if he has been able to render the magnificently beautiful tree as magnificently on his board.—They go on their way, and others replace them, but the artist paints on, the sleepers sleep and the brooders brood—a nursemaid comes and spreads dazzling white linen on the grass and places her charges in the sun and fresh air or up against the trunk of a tree; in the meantime, the sun has grown hot and the skies are blue, and a westerly breeze that has blown in over the sweltering city is surprised to find fresh forest green here; it stays a while to play in the branches of the white poplar.

Such fine, quiet times are to be had on sunny spring and summer mornings in the Prater, down river, where it loses its urban character.

But now, dear stranger, let us turn back from our sentimental wandering and, like those occasional couples and wavering groups, look to rejoin the crowds of people, returning at last to the city; for lo, the May sun is setting already, casting its gleam and fiery haze around the heights where Döbling and Grinzing and Nussdorf lie and the twin castles of Leopoldsberg and Kahlenberg, and if you were to catch a chill in the evening dew and night damp of the Prater, I would be most distressed, as it was I after all who led you down river to far-off, deserted spots.—But be of good cheer, we can already see the carriages driving up to the Lusthaus at the tip of the island on the water's edge,[*] and more and more hove into view further on. Now we can hear the music of the coffee-houses and then, finally, the music blaring out of the *circus gymnasticus*—and here is the same reeling up and down of carriages and the finery and splendour of the Hauptallee, the same deafening and bewildering ringing and clashing resounding from the Wurstlprater, the same surging and seething crowd that we left behind us. Weary now, you have only one wish, to escape from this knot of people; and you feel that the entire population of Vienna must either be here or else be in the process of leaving—but just look, we are already on our way up the seemingly endless Hauptallee, dazzled by the sunset which shines in our faces; now we are back in Jägerzeile and you see it crammed full of people, almost all of whom are going in the same direction—a mass of dark figures that blur before your dazzled eyes in the dust and sunset while the windows down the side of the street throw out a series of golden flashes. Tired and numb and bedraggled we finally arrive back from our jaunt, which we began with such enthusiasm, both seized with one and the same longing—and this shall be satisfied, only follow me; in a cool, airy room in my garden apartment, my wife awaits us

[*] An entertainment and refreshment pavilion originating from the 1560s which flourishes to this day at the end of the Prater Hauptallee.

and has set all that we need on the ready-laid table: fried chicken pieces on the tenderest of salads—a well-known Viennese speciality—and a carafe of really rather decent old Nussdorfer.[*] Refresh yourself, let us talk a while yet, and then off to bed with you, but be careful that you are not awakened by dreams and find yourself swept around and around in your bed by the crazy carousel of the crowds or else floating up and down the Prater in the midst of the masses in a ridiculously large carriage, wearing, perhaps, nothing but your undershirt, which would mortify you deeply.

Good Night.

[*] White wine from the Vienna Woods.

The Criminal

Veza Canetti

On Strasse des ersten Mai[*] the animal tamer Georg Burger
stands in front of his exotic show booth and pulls snakes
out of a box: poisonous (but only to other snakes), enormous (but with pretty patterns), modern, fat, and greedy
(but useful for ladies' handbags).

'This crocodile here is just a dainty little thing, but the
one inside is three metres long and 120 years old and
extremely dangerous! Just look at the mother ape feeding
her babies, you'll not see any monkey business here, come
in now, ladies and gentlemen, entry 50 groschen, children
half price!'

[*] 1st May Street, which runs through the centre of the Prater amusement
park, and was so named in honour of Labour Day by Vienna's first social
democrat city council in 1920.

Georgie Junior stands next to his father, the animal tamer, and watches him admiringly. He holds the snakes in his hand like pieces of string, lads stare open-mouthed. Georgie is so rapt he doesn't even notice the passers-by duck their heads and walk on or how woebegone his father is as he watches them go, for these are difficult times. Georgie knows nothing at all of any of this, how should he, the animal tamer Georg Burger doesn't let on to his boy how poor they are, and any minute now, we'll see just how he does it.

'Georg!' said Georgie dreamily (he called his father by his first name), 'can I go on the mountain train ride today?'

'On the mountain train ride, lad! Weren't you listening when I read you that article from the newspaper?—ah no, I remember, it was your mother I read it with—the mountain train ride came off its tracks yesterday! Twenty people fell out! You shouldn't even go anywhere near it, otherwise one might fall on you!'

'And the haunted castle?'

'The haunted castle! What, with all the ghosts and wicked demons and skulls and dragons and assassins that are in there! All made of wood, of course, but still they give you a terrible fright, today they had to carry an old lady out because she'd fainted!'

'And what will happen to me if I have a go on the electric automobiles, Georg?' Georgie was already enjoying himself.

'On the electric automobiles! Don't you remember the electric slot machine? Well, that was just a little shock; a shock from the automobile would tear through your whole body.'

'And the shooting range, Georg?'

'Last week a bolt shot backwards straight onto a lad's nose. Now he's walking around with a swollen nose.'

'And the Riesenrad?'* Georgie gazed wide-eyed into his father's kind face.

'Every third boy has to get out while it's going round and climb onto the roof, you have to do it to be allowed on the ride, don't even think about giving it a go ... but you'd better scram now, my lad, I have work to do.—Ladies and gentlemen! Roll up to see the only flying dog in Europe!'

Flying Dog is the name of an Indian chief, Georgie thought, and took off. He stopped in front of the haunted castle. Four fat women were wondering whether they should go in or not.

'Whatever you do, don't go in there!' said Georgie, 'an old woman had a stroke in there today! Dead on the spot!'

The women ran off horrified.

---

* Vienna's iconic ferris wheel.

His hands in his pockets, Georgie sauntered gracefully through the crowds to the mountain train ride. All of Class A from the high school were already there, waiting to have a go. Class B was in detention.

'I wouldn't get on there if I were you,' said Georgie mysteriously, 'a hundred fell off yesterday, covered in blood they were, some of them fell on me!'

The prefect who was about to buy the tickets was astonished at the boys' sudden change of mind, they'd been pestering him about the ride all morning.

'What shall we go on then, Georgie?' asked Peterheinz.

Georgie thought for a moment, serious. 'Well, the grotto train,' he suggested, for Georg had said nothing about that.

That was how the fusty old grotto train came to be full that day, and how its fusty old owner on the till got woken up. Cool as a cucumber, Georg got on with the other boys; the prefect noticed as soon as he counted and came to one too many, but Georgie slipped along with the others anyway.

'Aren't you that Georgie Hacker who wrote the diary of a bad boy?' Peterheinz asked him.

'I'm not called Hacker at all but Burger, like Georg, he has a really amazing animal show, there's a crocodile as big as the grotto train, but you can't hold your hand out to it, otherwise it'll eat you all up. It swallows a whole rabbit every day!'

The animal tamer Georg Burger was startled to see his lad roll up with a long line of boys, all of whom paid properly, with just a little discount because there were so many of them. After the animal show, they smuggled Georgie into the cinema.

The film was called 'Emil and the Detectives' but it had already begun a while ago, so they saw the middle first. Suddenly there was a commotion in the audience. A dolled-up woman stood with her arms crossed in front of a man who looked about helplessly and wasn't wearing a collar. Georgie liked him straight off, because Georg always said that there's no shame in not having a collar, although there often is in being rich. The programme seller went up to the man and told him to clear off.

'I only got here half an hour ago,' the man repeated, you could tell that he'd had to miss a meal to afford his cinema ticket.

'On your ticket it says five o'clock, you've got to leave now!'

'But he came in at the same time as us!' cried Georgie, upset, lisping a bit as he spoke; he was still only a very little boy, after all.

The programme seller took no notice of him, the man didn't move from the spot and the fussy lady waited with an unfriendly look on her face, then the manager came over from where he'd been sitting on the door.

'Get out of here at once!' he shouted at the man without a collar, and Georgie's heart ached at the way he looked around and nobody helped.

'Please, he can have my ticket!' Georgie cried, as loudly as his slender little body would let him. The other boys looked at him in admiration. But straight afterwards he was horrified. He didn't have a ticket himself, the boys had smuggled him in! His face went as red as fire.

'The tickets aren't transferable,' the programme seller said—luckily—and the manager shook the poor man by his shoulders and pushed him out. The audience hissed their approval.

'But he came in at the same time as us,' said Georgie with a dark look at the manager. 'I'm not staying here, lads. Georg always says you don't need to go looking at the bottom of the heap to find the criminals!'

The audience laughed, but Georgie paid no attention to all those people, he shook Peterheinz and the other boys by the hand and left the cinema with seven-league strides.

Ottakringerstrasse

Christine Nöstlinger

Ottakringerstrasse begins down at the Gürtel and ends up on the edge of town at the Vorortelinie.* I didn't know that when I was little. I thought Ottakringerstrasse was two tram stops long, from the Gürtel to Kalvarienberggasse. The houses on one side of the street belonged to Hernals, the houses on the other side belonged to Ottakring. I imagined that the boundary line between the two districts ran right down the middle of the street. It was shortly after the war, and there weren't many cars about. You could walk in the road—right down the middle. With one foot in Ottakring and one in Hernals. The Hernals foot was the home foot. I walked expecting my home foot

---

* The Gürtel is a semi-circular boulevard concentric to the Ringstrasse, marking the outer edge of the city's modern centre. The Vorortelinie train line runs along a section of the city's outer boundary to the north-west.

to feel special. The feeling never came, but a tram often rang its bell behind me and chased me onto the pavement, and the driver yelled out of the door—the trams always drove with open doors then—that I must be totally soft in the head.

Apart from me, there was a woman who used to walk down the middle of the road all the time as well. She had long, white hair, a wrinkled face like a monkey and bowed legs. On her left foot she wore a big brown lace-up shoe and on her right a small black pump. She pushed a pram that was riddled with holes. Sometimes there were empty bottles in it. Mostly it was empty. I would have liked to talk to her, but all she said was: 'Leave me alone!' When I saw that she also walked down the middle of other streets, I left her alone.

I can't remember the Ottakring side of the street any more. It had nothing to do with me. I had neither friends nor enemies in Ottakring. The Hernals side was all that was important. Nothing escaped my attention there.

There were four sorts of houses:

Three-storey blocks of flats with big windows, crumbling grey facades and battered stucco ornaments. I didn't like them. Most of all I didn't like their bare fire walls with the strip of toilet windows down the middle that rose up above all the other houses.

The two-storey houses—mostly with a couple of stone steps up to the front door and big yellow flagstones in the hall—were the most familiar. The house I lived in was like that. When I was out and about and got thirsty and wanted to drink at a bassena* in someone's hallway, I looked for one of these houses. My favourite was the one with the coloured fanlight over the front door. The fanlight was divided up into eighteen squares, six were purple glass, six were red, and six were made of frosted glass with flower patterns etched into it.

The one-storey houses were all built according to more or less the same ground plan. A wide gate and driveway in the middle, on one side of the gate a shop, on the other a storeroom and the caretaker's flat. The whole of the first floor was taken up by the owners' apartment, they also owned the shop below. I was envious of these houses. Their spotless, shiny windows, lace curtains and firmly locked doors seemed to me to guarantee prosperity and security and contentment.

And then there were the ruins. There were three of them on my bit of Ottakringerstrasse. Two, down by the Gürtel, didn't interest me much. They were little more than huge heaps of rubble with balconies sticking out of

---

* Water fountains in the shape of small, often ornate basins with a single cold-water tap to be found in the corridors and shared hallways of apartment houses in Vienna. The site of neighbourly encounters and gossip until this day.

them. I loved the other one, up by Steinergasse. It reminded me of the doll's house that had once been mine, before the bomb. In one of the gaping rooms on the first floor stood an old German cabinet, huddled up against the wall with barely a metre of floor left in front of it. I was absolutely sure it must be full of very precious things. Sometimes I climbed into the ruin. Then I was frightened that the doll's house might collapse on top of me. But the pleasure of scratching at the doll's walls on the ground floor was greater than the fear. There were countless layers of colour on the walls, one over the other. With patience, skill and a big hairgrip, you could scrape bare one layer after another. Behind pig-pink roses on a yellow background emerged stripes of blessed-virgin-robe blue and behind that cucumber-salad-green marbling with spring-violet-purple arabesques. I was sad every time the rain darkened my carefully revealed sample scraps. When they had dried out again, they were always paler than before.

People belong to the houses in my memory. To the ruins as well. Squinting Otti belonged to the doll's house ruin. He poked around in the rubble there every day looking for things. I was the only person he didn't chase out of the ruin. He was my friend. But we never spoke to each other.

Hansi was my friend too. He could always be found squatting on the doorstep of the house with the coloured fanlight. There were many days when he had the evil eye. You couldn't talk to him then, if you did, he yelled 'Beat it!' and slung a stone at you from his catapult.

The butcher from the one-storey house always stood in the open shop door and gawped in amazement whenever I marched along the street—right down the middle. Her nose, her ears, her fingers and her fat, drooping cheeks were purple with frostbite.

And right next door was Zwickl. When it was warm, he sat on a kitchen stool in the narrow doorway of the block of flats where he was caretaker. He had a single big yellow tooth. At the top in the middle. The tooth moved. By pressing gently with his tongue, Zwickl could push it about between his lips like a ciggy. And then there was old Mrs Wondraschek in the flower shop. There were several cats, a dog, and a toad in the shop as well as flowers. The toad mostly stayed in the ice-box. When Mrs Wondraschek's helper opened the box to get roses out, nothing was better than seeing the toad, with out-stretched legs front and back, make a huge leap onto the counter over the wreaths, bouquets, and basins full of cowslip. Old Wondraschek weighed more than a hundred pounds although she was very small and couldn't walk. In the mornings, her helper dragged her into the shop from her bed in the room behind and in the evenings she dragged her back again. Half an eternity ago, old Mrs Wondraschek had broken her leg. She didn't like the plaster cast and took it off with tongs and a hammer. Since then she had waited, binding wreaths, for 'me old peg leg to get better by isself again'. I often visited Mrs Wondraschek, because I liked her deep, husky voice that took on an especially tender tone when she used dirty words. 'Now then, yer funny bugger, mucky little squirt, how're yer keeping?'

My Ottakringerstrasse isn't there any more. Slowly, year by year, they took a bit away. And every time, someone who also belonged to Ottakringerstrasse in my memory disappeared. The old woman with the pram and the wrinkled monkey face was the first to go. Knocked over and killed. She didn't realize—as I did—that the traffic was different now, that no-one could walk any more with one foot in Ottakring and one in Hernals.

They put squinting Otti in a home. When the ruin was torn down and the rubble cleared away, they put up a billboard. Otti couldn't climb over it. And anyway, there was nothing left to find behind the billboard. So Otti stayed at home instead. And then the neighbours decided that it's not good for a growing boy to sit around in the flat his mother uses for her job as a prostitute.

The house with the coloured fanlight was pulled down
a year later. It was falling to bits because the owner went
up on the roof every evening and took a tile away, so that
the rain could get in. So that he could sell the land to a
building company. Hansi's parents, Hansi with the catapult, got a council flat at the other end of town. 'Lucky
them,' people said. But there wasn't much luck involved,
or so it seems. The whole summer, Hansi took the tram
from the other side of town to Ottakring. Once there, he
squatted in front of some house or other. All day long. And
he had the evil eye every day. The following winter, he was
gone. A couple of years later, people said he had been shot
dead by a night watchman during a break-in. The butcher's
house stayed where it was for a long time. Because she was
stubborn. She wouldn't sell. Even when she was very old
and the shop closed down. The contract of sale was signed
on the day of her funeral, though. Old Mrs Wondraschek's
house really did fall to pieces, all by itself. She took no more
care of it than she did of her leg. It was little more than a
ruin when they came to take her away in a specially-built,
wide coffin. Now there's a second-hand car salesroom
where her shop used to be. And in December they sell
Danish pine trees.

There are modern blocks of flats now on the site of the
butcher's shop, the house with the beautiful fanlight, and
my doll's house ruin. They have balconies. You can't use

them. The traffic is too loud. You can't even hang up washing. It gets dirty again.

The block of flats looked after by Zwickl with the moving tooth wasn't demolished until just this year. The owner let foreign workers live in it and 'wear it down' until it was 'ready'. Zwickl was admitted to Lainz. Three weeks later he died there. No wonder, really. After all, he was nearly ninety.

There are still a couple of old houses on my bit of Ottakringerstrasse. You hardly notice them when you walk past because the shop fronts are all new. All the windows at street level have disappeared.

Only the bars are left—one on every corner, because it's not the kind of area where banks want to open local branches. And the paint factory still stinks out the whole neighbourhood when the wind is in the wrong direction.

I don't know anything about the people who live in the new houses. They all live on the inside. They walk around outside as though they could live somewhere else entirely.

I put my hopes in the foreign workers. And their children. I see minute black-haired urchins carrying enormous net bags of beer bottles and don't see much difference to the way we used to get sent to the bars in the evenings—in the old days—to fetch tankards full of beer.

And last summer, the first ancient Mama with a black headscarf sat herself down on a kitchen stool in the narrow doorway of her block of flats. Whether squinting Otti pokes around in the rubble or little Milan rummages in the dustbins, I say to myself, it's all the same. Friendships and enmities are on display in Ottakringerstrasse again. People belong to houses once more.

But the boundary line, right down the middle of the road, means nothing to them. They run backwards and forwards, heedless of the traffic, and pick as many fights in Ottakring as in Hernals. Ask people 'what time is it, please?' just for fun the same way in Ottakring as in Hernals. Even go to get beer and milk and all that bread over on the other side. Home foot—no such thing any more.

Envy

Eva Menasse

Tichy had been standing there on the corner all along, a black scarecrow of a traffic policeman. To begin with he must have stood there alone in the blazing sun, looking somewhat odd in his funeral attire; to have got to his position against the garden wall in good time, he must have left the open grave earlier, much earlier. He probably left when the girls playing their guitars began to yowl like wounded animals, Bob Dylan or Leonard Cohen—I refuse to remember exactly what. That was the moment at which everyone present crept very deep inside themselves, out of grief, despair, or embarrassment. Embarrassment is perhaps a necessary part of every funeral as it guarantees that absolutely everyone takes a long hard look at their inner self, even nervous cynics like me, who, rather than displaying red-nosed weakness, prefer to stare round at all the others. Seldom does a better opportunity present itself.

The younger the deceased, the more torturous the event, if my theory is right. When a child has died, especially if it was a violent death, heaps of cuddly toys are now in vogue (do they get buried too?), at the funerals of youngsters there is handholding and uninhibited singing worthy of the churches of Harlem at the very least. Nowadays it's only old people who still get dignified farewells; in their case, death was only to be expected, there is no need for any ridiculous discharge of public emotion in the staging of a 'really personal' ceremony that nobody asked for.

If Tichy had crept off during the coyote singing, not even I would have noticed, even if he had been standing right next to me. I was totally aghast. Like a schoolboy caught red-handed, I tried to concentrate on the number of stitches in the side-seam of my shoes as the girls with their little piggy snouts reddened from crying actually sat on the grave, on the wooden planks that had been laid on the freshly dug earth so that the ladies, of which there were also quite a few present, would not get their black patent pumps dirty. The girls hunched their shoulders, lounging as though they were sitting on the horsehair futons they probably have in their shared apartments, in my day we had common-or-garden mattresses and probably a lot more sex. As they hunkered down and sobbed 'in the wind', their legs crossed in skinny jeans and guitars propped in between, I was suddenly immensely grateful for the metallic 'Ave Maria' that a mezzo soprano made-up in the gaudy colours of a fairground horse had belted out at my grandmother's funeral. Whatever. If Tichy had left at that point, at that mortifying moment of an embarrassment as absolute as death itself, then that was only to be understood. At least, wanting to get out of there, a hasty, unplanned escape would have been totally understandable, I would have sympathized, I would even have envied him his nerve. But in actual fact, he had a plan, a purpose that, given the occasion, was monstrous.

Kore, a *palais* in miniature run as a café and centre for the arts, is to be found on the edge of town at the end of a short lane that already has a positively rural air. Its cobbled surface leads straight to the café entrance, and you wouldn't think for a moment that it carries on after that. Kore stands there like a capstone, the end point of the lane. The wrought iron gate is already visible from a distance, and behind it, the gracefully crumbling Grecian columns and marble angels, the terracotta pots full of oleanders and rosemary. A secluded bower of playful romanticism, melancholic but not depressing, and therefore extraordinarily uncontroversial. But now I know, and will never, ever forget, that the lane continues, that there is another street number beyond Kore. What appears to be the natural forecourt of Kore, appropriate to its grandezza in the midst of the small, one-storey houses of the city's edge, is in actual fact still the lane itself. It bends round in a right-angle, carries on past Kore's shoulder-high brick wall and has another surprise in store behind.

Anyhow, Tichy stood there on the corner, looking as concerned as ever, nodding and murmuring and making little hand gestures along the garden wall, away from the entrance to Kore. That was how I saw him, and how all the others must have seen him as well. People are seldom so defenceless and trusting, so grateful for a loving hint as when they have only just managed to regain shaky control over their features, ten minutes after the funeral of a gifted, happy-go-lucky twenty-five-year-old.

I simply followed the people in front, I swear, just as we always believe that we are simply following the others, lulling ourselves into a sense of security, although all it takes is one inattentive moment and suddenly you find yourself participating in a perverse contest in which even Tichy is an accessory, harmless old Tichy with his crow's feet and thin hair.

Admittedly, I was distracted. Teetering along in front of me in lilac high heels was Ilka, my great, lost love;

well, her love for me had been lost a long time ago, mine for her had never completely disappeared. Although it's just as possible that the opposite is true. Perhaps she left as a way of saving herself from me, and I never actually loved her but just the idea of being crazily in love. I'm still mad at her, whatever the case. I didn't want to split up, and sometimes I still feel the urge to lay the blame for my discontented life at her feet, in their too-high shoes.

Ilka tottered over the cobblestones, clutching the arm of a man I didn't know for support. He was slim and athletic, not her type at all, as I saw at first glance; since she left me, she had always gone for father figures, older and heavier, jollier, with redder faces and more overbearing manners. Anyhow, I stuck to studying the ladder in Ilka's tights, which began in the hollow at the back of her right knee and ran seductively upwards. I can still remember how I wallowed in the idea that she must have scratched herself in the church just before and made the hole with her fingernail without noticing. If I, of all people, drew her attention to the ladder, she would hate it, as I knew just how touchy she was about that kind of thing. She always strived for lady-like perfection, although generally speaking, her charm had always been largely due to her unfinished air. And so I stared at the ladder and her cute ass and only briefly lifted my head, almost coincidentally; Tichy nodded to me with a sorrowful smile and a slight wave of the hand. That's why I too swung around the corner, behind Ilka, her sportsman and all the others, instead of carrying on straight ahead through the gate of Kore. I thought there must be a side entrance through the garden. That's what we all thought.

I didn't know Percass Haybach well. If you saw someone once on their tricycle, does that count as knowing them well? At the time when the circle around Heinz Haybach was the centre of my life, and Ilka and I got together because we had almost the same and the furthest way home after the long evening meetings, Percass and Rument were still children. Their real names were quite different, quite boring and respectable, Max and Moritz, Jakob and Josef, or Peter and Paul, I don't remember exactly. The strange names Heinz Haybach called them by were better suited to him than to the children themselves. They weren't actually any different from other small children: Percass, the older of the two, was the mischief-maker, Rument more the scaredy cat, a typical pair of brothers.

It was their father who was unusual. We, his students, secretly referred to him as 'wise old Hay', which was unbearably banal and certainly would not have pleased the man himself given the reverence apparent in the adjectives. Heinz Haybach was an exceptionally gifted scholar, the rising star of the university at that point; to us, he seemed the only professor worth studying under. He was the personification of that clichéd fictional figure, the teacher who does not court approval, but whose approval everyone seeks to gain—for whose sake we all studied harder than ever before, for whom we acquired knowledge we would never forget although we never needed it again, and whose bag we would all have felt honoured to carry, although none of us would have ever admitted it. When Ilka and I studied under Haybach no-one carried anybody's bag, of course, a decade and a half after 1968. But we booked the back room at Blaubichler's every Tuesday evening after his seminar, after we once found it already occupied and had to sit at a loud table in the front room of the pub. And Ilka, in a move that was typical, had a quiet word with the landlady to make sure that there was always pickled sausage on the menu on Tuesdays, for that was Haybach's favourite pub food. He never got it at home, he once let slip under his breath, that was the most we got in the way of private insights. Dunking his bread roll in the vinegar and hectically shovelling it into his mouth with chunks of sausage, he listened to Franz Gregor embark on one of his heated tirades. I referred to these contemptuously as Franz's 'doctrinae', they were improvised on the spot to provoke Haybach. Gregor was a couple of years older than us and worked as Haybach's assistant at the university, which no-one would believe today unless they had been there at the time. But not even Franz Gregor was born an *enfant terrible*, although that's what he'd like everyone to think now.

Haybach only ever took the time to eat while Gregor was delivering one of his harangues, but he still tried to interrupt him, to interject, to contradict without speaking, disagreeing, waving and stabbing with his forefinger. Haybach conducted, that's what we called it. We were familiar with the gestures from his lectures. He spoke as fast as a machine gun, but could still never keep up with the speed of his own thoughts, and because he considered his every move from every possible angle like a good chess player, he was never actually able to articulate all his arguments; his hands accompanied him as an instrument of doubt, refuting the speaker's opinions at times.

At the time I really hated Franz Gregor and his 'doctrinae'. In retrospect, this sentiment now seems childish. I probably wanted to be a little more like him, so hideously cultured and intellectually intemperate. He set up the most absurd theories with furious rhetoric only to laugh uproariously when they were pulled apart. He was the only one of us who seemed to be capable of challenging Haybach, and it was probably because of his entertainment value that we were able to boast of a regular pub meeting with our professor at all.

Sometimes we were invited back to Haybach's house. He owned a dilapidated villa in Dornbach, inherited probably, stuffed to the roof with books, pictures, rugs, and musical instruments. Frau Haybach kept herself to herself, only rarely did we hear Chopin from somewhere. She was a formidably beautiful woman of a type that ceased to exist a long while ago. The corpulent women in Doderer's novels conjured up a vague impression of her face for me, although at the time I could barely admit it to myself, because of the sexual implications, apart from anything else. Today I know so much more about both Doderer and Haybach's wife and can say with more precision: a dominatrix with the face of a Madonna. At the time, my twenty-year-old self cowered from her instinctively; Ilka's lilac shoes in imitation snake-skin would have been inconceivable on Frau Haybach's feet. Although younger then than Ilka is now, she was already a lady.

With a single exception, that was the only place I ever saw Percass Haybach—as a child in Dornbach. Percass adored Franz Gregor, and once, right at the beginning, widdled on his lap like a puppy. Gregor sat for the rest of the meeting in Haybach's dressing gown while his trousers were being rinsed out and ironed dry, and I managed to score my biggest ever laugh quite unintentionally by remarking that, at long last, his outside appearance harmonized with his inner world. My mockery was misunderstood as a compliment, being different was considered all-important. Another time Percass pushed his younger brother down something somewhere, and our discussion group in Haybach's library had to be broken off early for a trip to the hospital. While Tichy, at that point still his master's faithful servant, fetched Haybach's car, Ilka helped mop up blood in an upstairs room and the rest of us stood around listening to the duet of children's screams, not knowing how or when to take our leave. And a third time, probably in the run-up to Christmas, both of them were led in by their mother like circus animals to recite a long ballad. They both had bright red cheeks, Percass from stage fright, Rument from the humiliation. I can't really remember anything more.

But after all, people don't go to funerals for the benefit of the deceased. They either go for their own sake, needing closure for their own peace of mind, or else as a gesture of support for those left behind. Which was why, when the notice of Percass's death—prominent, large format—caught my eye in the *Presse*, there was really only one thing to be decided: whether or not I should ring Ilka.

'I kept asking myself the whole time if I should ring you,' Ilka panted as we ran back to Kore round the dogleg of the little lane, still bathed in mocking sunshine, 'but, you know, foolish pride.' She dug her nails into the sleeve of my suit; her ominous companion must already have been

conversing with Haybach—a complete stranger to him—
or vice versa. I only realized all of this later on, though. At
the time, Ilka's remark had at most the logic of displace-
ment activity. My attempt at an answer was no better:
'I saw Percass once later, as a adult.'

'Now you're just trying to make yourself important as
usual,' Ilka groaned (she didn't seem to be very fit) and
I retorted: 'That's why I didn't ring you.'

'Why?' she asked, as she pushed open the gate to Kore's
garden with her shoulder. She was looking so dishevelled
by this point—make-up smeared with sweat and tears, the
lilac feather in the knot of her hair bent, and, as I already
knew, a ladder in her tights up the inside of her thigh—
that I found her almost as irresistible as twenty years
before. This was the way she'd always been as soon as
she threw herself into the social fray, as steady as a rock on
the inside, but in total disarray from without.

'Because', I said and held her back in the door for a
moment by her sleeve, 'any old day I rang you, no matter
what the occasion, you would always have felt that I was
taking the opportunity to stage a performance.' Ilka gave
me an inquisitive look and blew a strand of hair out of her
face. I suddenly noticed that she had had the birthmark
on her right cheekbone removed. Of course she had aged.
Her laughter and doubt lines were visible now even when
she wasn't laughing or pulling a sceptical face, but she

understood me as well as ever. And as ever, she never gave up a fight before time. 'But any old day', she asked in a drawl, almost musingly, 'would presumably mean, not the days when the son of our professor coincidentally died in an accident, or your grandmother passed away or 9/11 . . . ?'

I let go of her and crossed my arms. The sideswipe about my grandmother hit home. When she had died, many years before, I had rung Ilka for the last time, knowing that her big heart would make her accompany me to the funeral. Afterwards, my grief and her solace naturally slid us into bed with one another, but that turned out to be a very bad idea. As I had to admit. And so I said, with an expression of mock-contempt, 'On any old day, dear Ilka, some rare animal falls down dead somewhere in the world for inexplicable reasons. You would have read it in the newspaper and cried out, "Stefan, how unbelievably melodramatic of you, today of all days!"' Ilka laughed out loud, and despite my best efforts, my face must have shown something of how happy that made me, for all at once, her mission came to the fore again, taking precedence, the greater good that does not permit delay. 'Get a move on,' she hissed, pushing down the door handle, 'poor Hay is already waiting.'

Kore was shockingly empty and quiet. I had only ever seen it overflowing before, full of clouds of smoke and the customers' voices, raised to be heard over the almost ear-splitting din of the espresso machine and cutlery clattering in the open-plan kitchen. Nevertheless, people were still prepared to wait in the entrance hall for a table, for the food was decent and the atmosphere 'quite delightful' as Ilka no doubt would have said. Normally there was a natural mix here of tourists, old ladies who regularly visit graves, raw youths in the first flush of love who had discovered a correspondence between their inner state and the melancholy, run-down Jewish section of the cemetery, and groups of students who, following lengthy expeditions in search of genre photos (angels and masses of ivy, always in black-and-white), were in desperate need of refreshment.

But today it was totally still and the air was fresh, sunlight sparkled on the coloured rhinestones of the craft market chandeliers, and there were spotless white cloths everywhere. On every table, photos of a roguish, laughing Percass stood propped neatly against little flower vases, no doubt just as they had been placed there that morning by one of the waiters. He's booked the whole place, I realized with horror, it was as touching as it was big-headed. The only movement was at the table in the bay window. Three people stood up, two remained seated. I recognized Hay-bach, who shook the hand of a tall man and patted him clumsily on the shoulder at the same time, then kissed a small, frizzy-haired woman on both cheeks before falling back onto his chair as though his legs had failed him. The couple moved towards us with a determined air, the man, frowning, gave a curt nod, the woman a curious, almost amused look. Then the door banged and they were gone.

'That was Rument,' Ilka whispered and pulled me to the table, right in front of Haybach. As though she had a dispatch to deliver, she said breathlessly, 'There's bound to be more people along any minute now,' and then she sat down and covered her face with both hands. Haybach nodded and made an attempt to stand, but I pulled a chair over and gave him my hand while he was still seated. 'Stefan,' he said, 'how nice to see you.' I was so overcome all I could do was give a vigorous shake of the head. 'I know, the occasion,' Haybach said, as though it was his job to comfort me, 'but such occasions are good for this kind of thing as well, you know.'

One of the best things about Haybach had always been that he was never really all there, although he was always so animated. Those dreadful moments of silence in which two people try desperately to think of how they can pull back as swiftly as possible from an unexpected chasm of embarrassment—you never experienced them in his presence because a significant part of him had always already gone on ahead, to the next discussion, the next thought. It could be annoying as a youngster, as you could never tell what he knew about his disciples apart from the area they were working on. Did he notice that Ilka was as pretty as a picture, but somewhat inhibited, with a red-hot sense of social responsibility, or did he think 'Molin, Ilka: émigré writing, Bachmann and the Vienna Group, good, good, but should really read a little more nineteenth century'? Did he have any idea of how screwed up and unhappy I actually was when he praised the 'poised, confident style' of my paper on Polgar? Did he foresee that his crazy assistant would soon become a famous poet? It was impossible to ask him any of these questions. His lovable, eccentric, frenzied manner seemed to create an extremely effective protective barrier around him. His was not a soul easily bared. I don't think he even had access to it himself. He only ever showed disappointment or annoyance within the bounds of his profession, and even then only in small doses. Perhaps he had become so intimately entwined with his job that a separate, private Haybach no longer existed. A Haybach who kissed his wife and dandled his children on his knee was simply inconceivable, although we had even seen him take his children on his knee.

'Stefan, this is my wife, Mia,' he said with casual geniality. I shook the hand of a woman who was similar in phenotype to the first Frau Haybach, but the opposite as regards her physical substance, if I can put it that way. She

was much drier, more brittle, not so fleshy. She acknowl-
edged me with an almost challengingly direct look; although
not exactly friendly, she at least paid me the respect of her
critical interest. Considerably younger than Haybach, she
nevertheless seemed unprepared to make capital out of the
age gap. She was barely made-up and dressed severely,
almost like a governess, and I wondered if this was solely
due to the occasion or whether she always screened herself
from the pleasures and colours of life in this way. I later
found out from Ilka that she was a high-powered finance
lawyer and had a blind child from her first marriage. Which
one could easily imagine.

Haybach poured me a glass of red wine and held out
the menu, which I refused with something like panic
although I was hungry. He shrugged his shoulders, murmured that the apple strudel was excellent, raised his glass
in our direction and took a gulp.

Then it was quiet for a while. I nearly wished myself
back at Percass's grave with the howling country girls, as,
for the second time that day, embarrassment took posses-
sion of me from the tip of my toes right up to my throat.
Even so, it still helped to imagine how the others might
feel. After I had taken a couple of mouthfuls, I hardly
dared look up, for I expected nothing less of myself than
to be the saviour of the whole situation. The great Haybach
was suffering deeply, as one would expect, and otherwise

there were only women and a stranger present. But the others didn't seem to expect anything more from me than my silent participation in this uncanny gathering.

Haybach, who still wore his smile of greeting as though he had forgotten to turn it off, stared ahead, probably seeing things that no-one would have envied him. Mia Haybach only had eyes for him, she observed him in his absent state like a doctor, attentive but calm. Ilka was still hiding her face like a child, and her escort was exercising an obviously inherent ability to blend into the background for all he was worth.

'Fifteen years', Haybach said at last, 'and no end in sight.'

'What actually happened back then?' Ilka asked, suddenly reappearing from behind her hands, with brutal courage. There it was again, her feminine instinct, that talent for hitting exactly the right spot while I searched desperately for innocuous topics of conversation. Just like the way she had split up with me, way back when, the extent of her pragmatism exceeding even that of her grief.

'I still ask myself the same question,' Haybach replied in leaden tones, as though he were suffering from nausea. At first he had remained silent, and even his hands were still; now he spoke as slowly as though he were listening out for the echo of every word. For once, he was not anywhere else, he had not hurried on ahead, his thoughts were stuck in the here and now, at the nebulous core of the whole drama. But it got even worse, for my role model—wise old Hay with the impenetrable ironic shield—revealed his private side. He actually tried to give Ilka an answer, whispering on with this strange new inflection: 'she hates herself, I don't know why.'

'What's that supposed to mean, "she hates herself"?' I threw in tersely, an inadmissible question that seemed to cast doubt on his statement, whereas in actual fact, I instinctively wanted to interrupt his disclosures, to prevent a confession, I wanted, damn it all, my old Haybach back again.

Haybach looked me in the eyes. Then he smiled a little, just like he used to when we didn't immediately understand exactly what he was driving at. He didn't look at Mia at all. Their relationship must play out on those lofty heights that I had always held to be the most gloriously grown-up and never managed to attain to myself, where there was no need to hold anything back when talking about ex-wives. Haybach continued to smile and began a careful retreat, 'I'm talking about destruction, Stefan, hard to understand, I know. At a certain point I had the impression that she couldn't stand the two of us together any more, or else that she couldn't bear herself in my presence.'

'Such a beautiful woman,' Ilka sighed, as though that had anything to do with it.

Haybach nodded. He had regained his composure. Just for an instant, he had lost the beat, but now he reverted to soothing us. He didn't waste a moment's thought on himself, he had always been a stranger to himself, of that I'm almost certain. In any case, he soon found his way back into his role as brilliant host, he became animated and waved his hands around, he turned on the wit and the charm, and I despised him and myself by turns, because, like an aged roué, he could now only give a poor imitation of the hero of my youth, and I had not been able to find it in myself to show compassion, even at such a moment.

Haybach called the waitress, a young girl who must have been wondering what on earth was going on. He ordered a platter of mixed cakes, 'just for the number of people here for the time being', and a bottle of sparkling wine. He had the bottle opened but did the pouring himself, five full glasses, handing them round almost expansively before lifting his glass and exclaiming: 'To my son Percass! I believe he was a happy man.'

We raised our glasses to the photographs on the flower vases, we drank to him and ourselves. For a brief second, I admired Ilka's friend, acquaintance or lover for his expression, which was above all reproach but at the same time revealed absolutely nothing of how he was feeling, a face like a blank sheet of paper. Perhaps that was what Ilka liked about him. Soon a second bottle of sparkling wine arrived. Haybach entertained us with anecdotes from his divorce, which to me sounded like case studies from 'Wit, Satire, Irony, and Deeper Meaning', a seminar of his that I had attended decades before. He had engaged an old friend whom he trusted as his lawyer, despite the latter's mental health problems; in the event, due to fits of depression, the lawyer was effectively unable to attend to the case for months at a time. 'We're going to give her everything,' Haybach exclaimed gleefully, and he laughed and beamed like a white-haired child, 'I said from the very beginning, "Bruno, we're going to give her everything she wants."' And she did want everything, that was the point of the story, the house in Dornbach, the whole inheritance, and whatever else there was to be had. Following the final verdict, they had gone to the Jakobinerwirt; Bruno had bought him a beer and, with the deathly bitterness of expression that came from his illness, murmured 'Heinz, now you have nothing left at all.' 'You did a good job, Bruno, I'm really grateful to you,' Haybach had apparently cried out in reply, 'I have nothing to reproach myself with, I didn't fight or sully myself, I bought my freedom with everything I had to offer. She couldn't ask for more than that.'

The door opened and three people came in, including one of the guitar girls. Ilka jumped up, a little too effusively, and I concluded from this that she must have felt less at ease than she had let on. Mia Haybach helped her husband to his feet, Ilka's colourless friend also stood up, but took a step back into the shadows. Stay sitting down, I said to myself, don't join in the play-acting.

The guitar girl rushed up to Haybach and took his proffered right hand in both of her own, the guitar dangling down over her shoulder. She lowered her head so that her blonde hair fell over her face and spoke to him in urgent tones. At the same time, she carried on shaking his hand as though it were holding her upright. As if to safeguard this intimate moment, everyone else began to make artificially loud conversation. Suddenly, someone grabbed me from behind, both arms around my neck, and exclaimed: 'Stefan, Stefan, I didn't recognize you back in the church!' It took me a while before I could see beyond the skin changes typical of alcoholism and recognize the face of a girl I used to study with, whose name I just couldn't remember. It wasn't easy to stand up, either, having been embraced from behind while sitting, but I managed it, I hugged and kissed a woman who looked like schnaps but smelt of baby powder, and who kept crying out in a shrill voice: 'Well I never, well I never!'

Ilka was at my side in an instant. 'Hey, Gaaaabi,' she said, settling on the first vowel as though it were a comfy sofa, probably to emphasize to me the enormity of my failure to remember, 'how did you manage to get away?'

'She gave a speech, that's why we're so late,' Gabi said, making a lunge for her companion and thrusting him in my direction. 'This is Rupi, my third. And before you ask, Andi's fine, thanks, but that's all I have to say about him, the bastard.'

Rupi, presumably Rupert, looked the typical jovial winegrower, by no means the snivelling, intimidated wretch that one might expect following such an introduction. Instead, his garden gnome smile indicated that he was the only other possible model: a nature as robust as the inside of a padded cell. Gabi was in good hands. The name Andi conjured up vague memories of a bland, skinny youth and suddenly I also saw the young, unsoiled Gabi before me, receiving her degree certificate with an eight-month bump. She had changed so much, more than I would have believed possible for any of us. Gabi and Andi, the first of us to become parents, hadn't they planned to become teachers? I had always arrogantly refused to attend any school or university reunions, instead of sacrificing myself once or twice, which would probably have spared me this attack from behind, or so it seemed to me in my growing superstition. I was beginning to see this whole day as an attack from behind, beginning at the moment I stepped through the cemetery gate in the harsh sunlight and recognized Ilka from afar.

Percass and Rument stayed with their mother, although not so very much later, enlightened couples began to find other models for the custody of their children following a divorce. Haybach had assumed that, although he would move out, nothing much else would change for the children, which was one of the reasons why he had let his wife keep the little villa without putting up a fight. But the first Frau Haybach, who had seemed so firmly settled in her way of life, began to toss and turn just a few months after the divorce. She sold the house, took Rument and Percass out of school in the middle of the year, and moved with them to the south of Lower Austria. Haybach did not have a driving licence, and to begin with, he travelled down there by bus and train to see the distraught children for a couple of hours in a cake shop. However, after he cancelled a visit because of an international conference, Frau Haybach refused to let him arrange further meetings. First she made up a series of excuses, and then she claimed the children didn't want to see him anymore. And one summer vacation, the day came when Tichy answered the phone under her number.

Eduard Tichy had been one of Haybach's assistants, a grey mouse who had made himself indispensable. In one of her poetic paradoxes, Ilka once said that he slaved with such a passion, he would have peremptorily commanded all the others in the bowels of the ship to take a rest as he could row fastest alone.

By contrast to Franz Gregor, propelled upwards by vanity before he threw in the towel, leaving a glamorous Romanian artist and their child behind him to embark on his triumphant rampage through the culture sections of the German newspapers, Tichy contented himself with marking essays, dragging charts and slide projectors into Haybach's lectures and taking care of administrative stuff. Despite all this, Tichy would never sign anything on Haybach's behalf, not even with the addition of 'p.p.' as his secretaries did as a matter of course. No, he gave everything he wrote to Haybach personally to be signed, although he did add an oblique line and 'ty' by hand after the date. It was like a nervous tick, a minuscule piece of proof that the work was all his. We joked at the time that one day, all the university's paperwork would bear this little 'ty' after the date: like Monsieur Hulot, he would eventually be inextricably entwined within a vast system, in a constant correspondence with himself that would never come to an end.

He stood in the way of his own career. When we began university, he was still rummaging about in his doctoral thesis, which he probably only ever finished because Haybach forced him to. Tichy was the kind of academic in whom arrogance and humility form a viscous mixture. Affable with students and helpful in every way, he had nothing but contempt for the big names and their grand designs. He could never see anything good in new ideas because he hated their originators—along with their grand designs—for having dared at all in the first place.

As a logical consequence, he only ever chose topics for himself that were 'sisyphoric', to use one of Haybach's terms. He planned to write his second book about nothing less than representations of the intellectual in literature. When we lay in bed after my grandmother's funeral, smoking and chatting to cover up the failed sexual connection and misunderstandings that had just taken place, Tichy anecdotes were a welcome lifeline. Finally I was even able to make Ilka whoop with laughter—by imitating this unfortunate figure. She in her turn told of a symposium where his theories on *The Magic Mountain* had been torn to pieces, although the paper, people wickedly claimed, had been nothing but a small selection from the immense preparatory studies for his planned book. 'Actually nothing more than the lecture-length elaboration of a footnote from the first paragraph of the introduction, shortly before he gets round to explaining what it is he actually wants to do,' Ilka mocked. And then we discussed like hysterical teenagers what on earth it might be that had attracted the stunning Frau Haybach to such an old duffer.

We had heard about the Haybach divorce, of course, although nobody knew any details. Haybach had disappeared off abroad, and Tichy had been seen accompanying the beauty to the theatre, that was all. For a little while at least, most people probably assumed that he was merely continuing his major-domo role at Haybach's command, for anything else was essentially unimaginable. But he had in fact moved to the south of Lower Austria, and sometimes he could now be seen lifting her fingertips to his lips in the theatre box.

Heinz Haybach was more or less excluded from his sons' youth. Ilka, whose children seemed to be of a similar age and who found the thought of this 'maternal cock-up' hard to bear, appealed post festum to the judge, lawyer, and youth services in Kore, but Haybach, with unworldly forbearance, reminded her of King Solomon. Whoever demands that the child should be cut in two with the sword...

'King Solomon let you down when it came to making sure that reason won the day,' I said more sarcastically than I intended, but with a dismissive wave of his hand, Haybach merely answered: 'Reason does not aim to win, Stefan. It was about the children.'

'Who must have held it against you later that you didn't put up more of a fight for them,' I retorted, only to intercept a warning glance from Ilka. But Haybach

didn't need protecting. As it was impossible to get everything right in any case, he replied, all one could do was to
avoid anything that was patently wrong.

At this point Gabi joined in with a vengeance and in
lurid and indecent detail, pulled us down with her into the
depths of her divorce. Unintentionally, but categorically,
she refuted the theory Haybach had hinted at, that there
must be such a thing as superior reason. She was living
proof that most people, to the detriment of themselves and
all around them, only know the story of their own injuries
and don't believe that any other tale is worth telling.
Bizarrely, she seemed to believe she was Haybach's ally, a
fellow victim of ex-partners turned monsters and a justice
system that was misguided to say the least, if not downright manipulable.

This was all far too much real life for me. I stood up
and went to the toilet to give my hands a very thorough
wash. I looked at myself in the mirror, discovering a tiny,
dark-red mark on my collar that could only come from
Ilka's lipstick. For once I didn't care—this was the right
occasion for displaying scars, if ever there was one. When
I returned, Gabi's accusations still rang round the room.
I went to the bar, ordered myself a schnaps and stayed put.
Mia Haybach, also on her way back from the toilet, discovered me there. 'May I join you in the lifeboat?' she

asked, and I pushed a stool towards her. She gestured at my schnaps, nodded to the waitress and sat down.

'Even you are deserting your husband now?' I asked provocatively. 'I always thought his way of handling it was right,' she answered earnestly, 'it's only lately that I've begun to ask myself whether it's really possible to be so sure.'

We clinked glasses. She tossed back the schnaps in a single draft, banged the empty glass down on the bar and ordered a bottle of still mineral water. Sunk in thought, she watched as the waitress searched—still water didn't seem to be much in demand here. I wondered whether the preference for carbonated water was linked to the cemetery, tingling life bubbling up, reviving the senses, and asked myself if I was already drunk.

While he was still living in the village, Percass seemed to have taken things out on Tichy as much as he could, while the timid Rument became all the more attached to his mother. 'You're just like your father,' the first Frau Haybach is supposed to have said to Percass once during an argument. 'I should hope so!' the nearly seventeen-year-old replied. And that was precisely the point, Mia Haybach told me: Percass, so much like his mother in appearance, always reminded her of his father in his ways, strong, self-confident, either loved or feared wherever he went. 'You saw the crowd at the cemetery,' she said and pointed out of the bay window, 'half of his year at university, all friends, disciples, girls in love with him.'

Percass apologized to Tichy later for having tormented him as a teenager. But he never managed to win over his brother again. For Percass was obsessed with the idea of converting Rument. He had to be made to admit that their mother had done them wrong, intentionally alienated them from their father, exiled them to the dreary village, indoctrinated them, resorted to emotional blackmail with the heart and nerve complaints that always appeared at just the right moment. But Rument would have none of it. He didn't want to know, he insisted that their different viewpoints should be equally respected, that their mother had been injured too and that intervention and judgement by the children was not only unseemly but also 'no earthly use', for the truth generally lay 'somewhere in between'. Such phrases goaded Percass into appealing to Rument's intelligence, which didn't improve the situation. Soon Rument refused to have such discussions at all, and the contact between the two brothers became increasingly sporadic. That was the opposite of what Percass had wanted, and despite all his charisma, he suddenly began to yearn for his little brother, his closest ally.

Wars sometimes draw equivocal frontlines. Percass as his father's, Rument as his mother's child; Percass the rebel, Rument the conformist. But you could also see it all the other way round, Mia said. Rument had learned to look for ways to bring people together, Percass for ways to keep them apart. Their natural tendencies were probably the exact reverse.

'Are you a psychologist?' I asked her bluntly, and she smiled, cooler now, and replied, 'It always helps to try turning things the other way out, like putting on a glove.'

Heinz Haybach was of no help to Percass. Rument only phoned his father on his birthday and at Christmas, on both occasions unfailingly around ten in the morning. The stilted felicitations were meant as a humiliation, or at least as a protest. But still Haybach was not prepared automatically to support Percass's attempts at reconciliation. 'He probably sensed the fantasies of omnipotence that lay behind them,' said Mia, who to me was beginning to seem like Haybach's divine destiny in wifely form, a perfect fit, a high priestess of imperturbability.

Haybach had told Percass that it wasn't all as simple as he thought, 'there is very little that is simple, almost nothing in fact, and certainly never anything that is interesting,' Haybach, the university lecturer, had always preached. 'All you're doing is strengthening Rument's convictions,' father instructed first-born, 'no-one can think about anything properly until they have the room in their head to do so.' As a result, the two of them were not on the best of terms either when Percass, who didn't drink himself, got into the car of a drunk driver early one morning after a party and lost his life in an accident caused by the latter.

A middle-aged man came out of the kitchen, dark rings under his eyes and five o'clock shadow on his chin. He was wearing a clean white jacket and headed discreetly but determinedly for Frau Haybach. Head bent slightly forward, he took up position next to her bar stool and asked in a low voice if it were possible to clear up and open again for the public, as it seemed no-one else was going to come. He really was dreadfully sorry, but he would have to ask for the basic rate of €400 for booking the whole café as the takings had not made up the sum in the usual way, he was sure that madam would understand. 'But of course, my dear Herr Opletal, please feel free to open again,' said Mia Haybach in a friendly voice, 'thank you so much, and that will all be absolutely fine.' The landlord nodded vigorously, relieved, and hurried to assure her that the minimal consumption that had taken place, the sparkling wine, red wine, and cake, would of course be included in the overall price. This seemed to irritate Mia Haybach after all, and she made a move to turn back to me, but Opletal hadn't finished with her yet. 'What is it now, my dear fellow?' she asked, and he murmured: 'The photos, the flowers, do you want me, should they . . . you see what I mean?'

Mia laughed. 'My God,' she said, 'such problems.' And then she asked the man just to leave the flowers where they were, he was more than welcome to carry on using them, but he should pack up the photos for her. She said 'pack up' just like people used to when it was still the done thing in most places to take uneaten food home with you. Probably the older visitors to the cemetery still did, using the usual excuse that it was for their dog.

At the Pomegranate I would have still dared to ask, as I used to in my childhood, carrying home from Sunday lunch half a schnitzel in silver paper from the 'restaurant', as people used to call any greasy old café in those days, already full of joyful anticipation of my evening meal. All you had to do was point at the leftovers on your plate when you paid the bill and say 'pack it up, please' and then the waiter brought the aluminium foil, which in those days was still known by its old, familiar, misleading name. The Pomegranate, which you would never have found if you didn't know about it already, was exactly that kind of place.

It appeared unexpectedly as soon as you reached the end of Kore's garden wall, at the point where the cobbled lane actually came to an end. The painted sign 'Welcome to the Pomegranate—proprietors: the Kern family' marked the corner of a far bigger building, probably a farmhouse, that looked dilapidated and uninhabited. Behind it, the fields began. Nothing had been renovated for generations, the Kern family didn't even seem to have bothered whitewashing, and every film set designer and social historian would have kissed their feet for it. A low, L-shaped room, wrought iron coat hooks on the dark, wood-panelled walls, scoured wooden tables and hand-carved beer-mat stands—if Ilka and I had had to choose between the two places as students, we would definitely have gone for the Pomegranate, in the meantime however, our preference had changed for the more controlled elegance of Kore, which, compared to this uncompromising venue, was almost *chi-chi*.

Nothing, however, was more unsuited to the elegance and appearance of the first Frau Haybach. And that was what proved to me that she had chosen it solely out of malice. She had used the tricks of its topography for her own ends, not wishing to fight openly for guests for her rival funeral feast, but simply to lure them into a trap.

At the end of the afternoon, as we headed harmoniously for the tram together like we always used to do because Haybach and Mia—worryingly—wanted 'to stay a little longer', Ilka tried to substitute cowardice for my verdict of malice. As if that were any better. She assumed, she said, that Frau Haybach had had no confidence in either herself or Tichy to redirect the congregation of mourners openly, that is to say, within sight of the grave. 'That would have caused a scandal,' Ilka said and I cried out, 'As if it wasn't one anyway!' 'At most a secret scandal,' she countered, seeming to think that she could put her arm through mine now that she had sent her acquaintance home in his car, 'which by the way, is as paradoxical as a still birth'.

And then she pulled the twice-folded death notice out of its envelope; I had never seen it as I had rung Haybach to offer him my condolences and had been invited to Kore on the phone. Printed on thick, expensive paper with a jagged edge, the text concluded 'in deepest mourning, Heinz and Ulla Haybach with Rument and Joana'. No Mia, no Tichy, but Rument and his wife under 'with' as though they were still children. The most barefaced pretence of an erstwhile, intact state of affairs, unfortunately broken apart by sudden death. Above the small print, which outlined suggestions for how money could be better invested than in buying wreaths, there were clear instructions: 'Following the funeral service, the family invites everyone to the arts centre café in Kore.' 'You see,' Ilka said, and began to cry bitterly as she walked, 'that was what they had agreed in advance.'

Of all the people present, only she had realized what was going on. So maniacally obsessed with observing her surroundings that she often didn't notice the ladders in her tights or her own body odour, Ilka, this heart on legs who touchingly believed herself to be a schizophrenic cynic, had seen and understood everything: the way Tichy had disappeared early and stood helpfully on the corner, the inviting gestures towards the Pomegranate that didn't tally with the invitation, and the fact that 'proprietors: the Kern family' were not in the least surprised by such a large party of mourners. But unlike myself and probably most other guests who noticed the change of venue, she did not see the latter as a good sign, but as downright suspicious. She did stop to consider that not everyone is as pedantic as she is and that a death in the family is almost bound to mean that small alterations don't always get communicated on time, but she knew Haybach. Yes, she really did seem to know Haybach well, for she sensed that he would never have left Tichy standing out in the sun like that.

And although she was squeezed into a corner bench and found it embarrassing to have to ask everyone to stand up again, she couldn't stand the uncertainty. She climbed on the bench and pushed her way out, crouching down behind the backs of the other guests, doing her best not to skewer anyone's behind with her high heels, and apologizing in a whisper the whole time. Her escort, the pale-faced IT expert, had not been able to find anywhere to sit down, she took his arm and pulled him away with her. And as more and more young people streamed into the

Pomegranate, silent, weeping, or hysterically noisy, Ilka made her way in the opposite direction, together with the acquaintance who had no real part in any of this. Trudging past the busily waving Tichy and hardly able to believe her own suspicions, she went to check in Kore.

Less than ten minutes later, as she stormed back to fetch me and the few others that she still knew, Tichy had left his post. His work was done, the lane was empty. The sun was high in the summer sky, Percass lay young and immobile below the ground, Rument was preparing himself for his second funeral feast in the Pomegranate and their parents were, at last, even further apart than most other couples ever manage to get, despite their best efforts.

Six-nine-six-six-nine-nine

Doron Rabinovici

Some days the phone never rings.

Sergio listened. He sat in front of his synthesizer. He waited. The computer purred, connected to the music machine by a sound module. Three horizontal electronic lines on the monitor made up the sound diagram. A spermatozoon of light emerged on the right only to swim to the left, disappear, and flash up again where it had come from.

Sergio flipped a couple of switches, let his middle finger sink onto a key, and immediately the humming of a dragging heartbeat pulsed, a slow samba. Larghissimo. A sound pattern erupted on the monitor, wavy peaks wandered from right to left, imitating frequency and volume in colours, only to scurry straight off the grid again. Sergio let his fingers—hesitant, halting—trickle over the keyboard. As he played around, a motif slowly formed, like a crystal in a chemical experiment. Suddenly, all three lines of the diagram broke up and hot drops sprayed high. Sergio tried to find his theme in variations. A chord whittled here, a triplet placed there, but nothing worked, the structure blurred, wouldn't condense.

He broke off playing, shook out his wrists and looked over at the telephone. The computer fan and hard disk purred in quiet revolutions.

He had moved into this solitary garret in the suburbs several months before. As she struggled with the old lock, the caretaker said: 'I'm telling you, this apartment's just made for a musician. Peace and quiet to make as much noise as you like, right? The owners—died a while back, God rest their souls, first him, then her—got the apartment decades ago from a musician...but I was just a kid then. She was a singer, an opera singer. Her piano's still here, but she had to go.' Sergio had had to break the door open.

He had the old Börsendorfer tuned and set up his studio as soon as the wiring had been re-done.

For months Anja had been trying to persuade him to find a second home, somewhere he could compose without being disturbed. The harmony, the accord he needed to create polyphony evaded him in the apartment they shared. It was also impossible to make music at night as the neighbours forbade all noise—as did Anja, who worked at the Physiological Institute during the day.

Their first year together they had lived in his apartment in the city, and to start off with, after his move to the garret studio, Sergio still used to go to Anja's place in the centre every evening, but now they lived divided up three ways, commuting between Anja's and his two addresses. They rarely saw each other and spoke on the phone several times a week.

He reached for the receiver. Before he could even dial, he heard a woman's voice: 'Hello?'—'Hello?'—'Sorry, is that six-nine-six-six-nine-nine?'—'No, I'm afraid this is five-one-three-seven-seven-nine-eight.' Both fell silent, then she asked: 'Does that mean you don't want to talk to me?' He laughed and said: 'On the contrary. I am all ears. Finally got someone on the line,' and she replied: 'Oh really? Then I'm hooked.'

Her voice ensnared him like full-bellied string music, a deep, quiet legato. This was not the muted calm of modern digital devices, a rushing sound swept through him down the wire, accompanied by a distant echo and, now and then, resounding clicks. Crackling noises flared up like small explosions on old shellac. The timbre of the woman's voice had not been thinned out by all the cables but occupied its own space, like a reserved atmosphere not to be dissipated by any electronic refinement.

'Viola', she called herself, and as he listened to her voice, it seemed to him all at once that he could see her too. Dressed in a light robe, she sat on the edge of her bed with the telephone on the floor between her feet, leaning over it and playing with the cord. While she listened to him, smiling, she brushed her hair back from her forehead. He could see it clearly. He saw her wide face, firm throat, low neckline, and even her breasts as she leant forward over the phone.

She said: 'I don't know. I think I wanted to talk to you because I liked the way you didn't answer with your name and number. Every call is an assault. You shouldn't have anything to do with anyone who doesn't realize that.'

'That's right,' he said and thought of Anja. She had never understood how to start up a conversation on the telephone. For two whole weeks, he had always been the one to ring her, the young doctor he had met at a New Year's Eve party. On the fourteenth of January, she had dared to make her first call and had greeted him, her lover, with 'Hello? Who's there?' His brusque reply had been: 'Who's that and who do you want to speak to anyway?'

Later she started her calls with: 'Hello? Sergio?'—'Who wants to know?'—'Hey, it's me.' For some time now, Sergio had suspected that Anja was not, would not be the woman who hooked him, with whom he wished to stay on the line.

Viola: 'I'll ring you.'—He said: 'We could meet up,' but she just said: 'I'll ring you, Sergio.'

The next day he had the computer play back the sounds he had saved, the soundtrack to date. He followed the music using the score it had printed. Anja still hadn't rung, but it didn't bother him, he hoped to speak to Viola again instead.

He reached for the receiver. Six-nine-six-six-nine-nine. A woman answered: 'Hello?' but before Sergio could say anything, a third person on the line said suddenly: 'Anja?'—'Yes.'—'It's me, Anja.'—'Peter?'—Sergio listened, astonished, to the conversation.

Sergio remained silent, ran his hand through his hair, hearing all the endearments, recognizing all the assurances that until recently had been addressed to him. 'And Sergio?' Peter asked, and they fell silent. All three. Anja said: 'This evening. It's over. He's known it for ages somehow, and it won't really bother him much anymore.' Slowly the conversation retreated into the distance, and words from the last couple of years rose up in him. When the other two put the phone down, the connection cracked, as though he could hear his larynx breaking and suddenly there were tears in his eyes.

He was still holding the receiver to his ear, the line chirruped, and then her voice reached him, silkier, lighter than the day before. Viola said: 'Hello, Sergio!' He winced, faltered, hung up, ashamed.

He picked the phone up again straight away, and before he could even begin to dial, Viola said: 'Hello, Sergio! Viola speaking.' Silence. 'Hang on...I don't understand. What's going on here? First Anja and that guy, and now you again. Are you my dialling tone now or something? Did you call me? Because the phone didn't even ring.'

Viola explained: 'I have a connection. I'm in the network. I can reach you anytime, I can listen to you even when you've put the receiver down. I can put you through to any number.'

'Viola? Are you somewhere in the same house or what? On an extension?'—'Am I an extension?!—Were you crying, Sergio?'—'How do you know?'—'Your voice,' she answered. 'Right all the way down the line,' he conceded.

Once again he thought he could see her. She was perched on a sofa, her pointy knees under her chin. She held her back upright, her hair, red-brown, fell like a curtain, vertically, only her face lay aslant on the receiver in her left hand.

After a conversation of two hours Sergio asked: 'Do you work on the central switchboard?' but she replied, 'No. I already told you: I'm in the network.'—'What's that supposed to mean? I want to see you, Viola.' Viola laughed. 'Oh, really? So I'm not just an extension after all?'

Afterwards she told him to take the telephone cord in his hand, make a loop, then a knot and pull gently. After he'd done all of this without protest, he asked: 'What now?'

'Well, we've just confirmed our connection,' she said, gave a short laugh, added, 'till tomorrow,' and hung up, leaving him down, but—carefully replacing the receiver with the knotted cord on its cradle, he was instantly soothed again.

The next morning he reached for the receiver once more. This time, as soon as he heard her voice, he thought she must have black hair. He wanted to know: 'What do you look like?'

He wanted to see her at all costs, but she warned: 'Don't ask me that. Do you hear? Promise you don't want to see me. Promise it now. If you want to stay with me there's no going back. Don't you understand? I'm in the network, grown together with the line. The cables sprout out of me. I was annexed, caught in the wires. I had all the contacts run via my number. It was about connections. It was necessary. That was how I got caught in their net. Do you understand?'

'No,' Sergio whispered, and Viola tried again: 'I spoke on the phone for hours with people in far-away places, and gradually, hair-fine fibres formed between the receiver and my skin, fibres that got thicker until wiry connections grew out of my fingertips, the palms of my hands, ears and hair. Do you get it now?'—'No,' whispered Sergio. 'I want to touch you.' Viola spoke again with a threat, a plea, but also a kind of triumph in her voice: 'Listen to me, Sergio. But don't look round. Listen, Sergio,' and then he heard her voice, her breath, and all at once, wires began to sprout out of the holes in his telephone, connecting themselves to his head like electrodes or else flowing into his hearing. She had connected him to the current.

All at once he feels her thighs straddling him, feels her naked skin and her wetness, although he knows he has clothes on; he smells her sweat, he tastes her mouth, he feels her breast, strokes her waist and hears her panting.

He is girdled about, her nails in his back, in his neck. He feels her sitting on him, taking him in, rocking, slowly. When he closes his eyes, he knows he is with her, but when he looks, he doesn't see her. When he opens his eyes, it all seems to be a sensory illusion, seems as though she is deceiving him or doing it with someone else, someone who is still him. When he sees that she is nowhere to be seen, not anywhere, he lurches around, blind, blinded.

He closes his eyes.

Afterwards. The wires had detached themselves from his head, withdrawn into the receiver, as though they had been rolled in, cleared up, brushed aside. They had both been silent for a long time, until he dared to open his eyes again and saw that it had become dark and cold. Sergio said: 'Viola, I have to see you.' And then the connection was lost.

She didn't ring. In the morning, he reached for the receiver and dialled six-nine-six-six-nine-nine. He listened to the number not available tone that followed. Directory enquiries knew nothing about the number, but the operator recommended him another one to ring.

By midday, he had got through to someone who should be able to help, a retired civil servant, hobby historian, an archivist of the telephone network.

'Six-nine-six-six-nine-nine? Just a moment.—The number was discontinued decades ago,' the old man explained. Sergio insisted: 'I phoned this number only yesterday,' but he still didn't budge: 'Absolutely impossible. The number was replaced.'—'The number was replaced?'—'But of course', said the man, and Sergio asked: 'Whose name was it listed under?'—'Let's see. One Viola Goldfarb, opera singer.'

Sergio asked for the new number that had replaced the old one.—'Five-one-three-seven-seven-nine-eight.'— It was his.

Sergio hung up. Night had fallen. No light in the room. He switched on his computer and the sound module. The concerto was finished now. With one key he called up the saved music, sat down at the Börsendorfer and played against the grain.

Some days the phone never rings.

Merry-go-round

Joseph Roth

The March sun, full of promise, coaxes the occasional merry-go-round out of the ground in the Vorstadt.* You're taking the tram down an endless street, past grey tenement blocks, there are fewer and fewer shops, the children get dirtier. Just before the viaduct the street gives a sudden yawn, opening its jaws as wide as they will go, and leaves a space, a bit of grass or whatever. You can't really tell what it's supposed to be. The city hasn't decided yet whether this is where it should end or not, there is such an air of hesitant uncertainty to everything—to the fence, which would rather lie straight down on the ground instead of feeling obliged to remain

---

* The area between Vienna's historic centre and what used to be its outer defensive wall (now between the Ring and the Gürtel, districts two to nine).

bent but upright; to the grass that sprouts out of the ground, unsure about whether it belongs to the grey of the street or the green of spring; to the people, who have city slicker ties around their necks and the boots of country dwellers on their feet.

This is where the merry-go-rounds begin.

The square bathes, swims in spring sunshine. As though whole buckets of it had been poured out onto the ground. Children poke around in heaps of dirt. A philosophical poodle ponders why there should be no flies on such a sunny day. A couple of railway men, pipes in their mouths, stand like blue lines drawn through the scene. They smell of coal dust and yearning. A pack of youngsters are taking a break on the edge of the grass.

In the middle, the merry-go-round, locked up with wire.

A thick tree trunk branches out at the top. It looks like the skeleton of an umbrella, but a thousand times bigger. Wooden seats swing at the end of long chains. And ten lads stand on the top in a kind of merry-go-round attic, pulling on the chains: round about and round about again. Whoever has helped pull for half a day can have ten goes for free, one after the other.

Herr Rambousek, merry-go-round director, is an imposing figure. An elephant tooth dangles on his silver watch chain. Herr Rambousek has a suit of blue corduroy velvet. He brandishes a horsewhip—Hoppla! Crack! Didn't you notice?—in his right hand. And after every ride, he blows a short, sharp blast on his whistle. The lads in the attic stop turning. The circular movements of the seats cease at the whistle's command. Then Herr Rambousek—Hoppla! Crack! Horsewhip in his right hand, sports cap in his left— goes to collect the fare from his passengers, twenty heller a ride.

Over the other side, a hurdy-gurdy churns out polonaise at a gallop. Racing bass notes throw themselves, puffing and panting, on the young squeaky notes. Rough and tumble ensues. Dreadful things must be happening in the belly of the instrument. The minor tones are the losers. Inevitably. Was only to be expected. When Herr Rambousek whistles, they all fall to the ground, major and minor, low G and high C sharp, all mixed up together.

Herr Rambousek has a family. They all live together in a caravan on wheels. Herr Rambousek travels far and wide and is always ready to go. All he has to do is hitch up his two horses. And then he climbs onto the driving seat— Hoppla! Crack! Didn't you notice?—He's gone!

I'd love to know what kind of passport Herr Rambousek has, and how he manages all the borders.

There's a baby in the caravan, you can hear it cry. Frau Rambousek is in a negligée—it's only four in the afternoon after all.

With a theatrical flourish, she pours dirty water out of a basin across the square. The poodle is startled out of its reverie. Its chain of thought is soaked now. It trembles, dripping nerves and water.

Washing hangs on long lines. The wind blows out the intimacies of the Rambousek family. The square looks like a sailing ship.

A faint aura of half-forgotten romance lies over the whole scene. Tramping the country roads. Once I saw three gypsies, it was a night in May...

Warm March air rises from the ground, you can smell blossom somewhere. The baby is still crying, the hurdy-gurdy roars and rages.

And Herr Rambousek, always on top, pirouettes with light feet over the burdens of day-to-day life—Hoppla! Crack! Didn't you notice?—calling: Roll up! Roll up!

Out for a Walk

Arthur Schnitzler

Embers of June sun burnt down slowly. Out there, way beyond the outer wall, a long row of tall, identical houses stretched out, glistening an ugly whitish yellow. Men in shirtsleeves stood at the many open windows, following the clamorous tram with vacant eyes; blowsy women in loose chemises stared into the distance. Grimy children played noisily in the streets; and on the dull green meadows that began here and faded into gentle hill country further out, there were common folk who yearned for fresher air without knowing it: little boys and girls rolling on the ground or running to and fro, soldiers smoking cheap cigars with idiotically cheerful off-duty faces, street-walkers in twos and threes laughing loudly as they strode over the fields, and the occasional solitary wanderer who had ventured out to savour the atmosphere of this peculiar no-man's land where the city gradually comes to an end, its raw, drawn-out, fearful panting ceasing in a weary, thankful sigh.

That was how the four friends came to be out there today. The last embers of sunset died down, cool shadows crept up the walls, slowly, until they disappeared on the roofs. All that remained, way out on the last buildings, was a reddish, aching glow. And they walked on to the final houses. The road came to an abrupt stop; this was where the city ended. They turned and looked back at the cloud of dust and vapour out of which the streets seemed to crawl with an enormous effort. They stood still.

'Curious!' said Hans. 'When I lived abroad for a couple of months two or three years ago, I may have missed the Ring, our theatres, the Rathaus, perhaps a couple of pretty Viennese girls and maybe all of you a little bit, but I only felt true homesickness, the kind that moves you to tears, when I thought about places—like this. This is where Vienna's soul is, if you ask me—here, where it becomes so still . . . so forlorn . . . '

'You'll pardon me for remarking', said Max, 'that this is exactly where the city ceases to have a character of any kind. You perhaps have a half-conscious memory that you associate with this place, and that's what gives you such a strong feeling of home right here. Or perhaps it's because the whole city lies at your feet here, and you can see it in a more orderly fashion than when you wander through its streets. Or maybe your impressions of it only begin to take effect here, when everything around you falls quiet and still.'

'But perhaps none of these reasons apply,' Stefan cut in, 'because it's not necessarily the characteristic features of your home town that you love. In fact, it doesn't even have to be something that actually exists at all. Take me, for example: I've discovered that the things I love best about Vienna are all long gone. I'm fond of the houses from 1760 that were demolished years ago, the Viennese ladies of 1820 who passed away long since, and the waltzes by old man Strauss, the sad ones that nobody plays any more. And when I stroll around the Ring in the springtime feeling at one with the world, it's clear to me right away that I'm actually a gentleman from 1870, seeing everyone else as I would see them on pictures many years later.'

'That's all just your imagination!' Fritz exclaimed. 'Nothing but another ploy to make life worth living. Every now and then, we contrive to persuade ourselves— in the pleasantest ways possible—that we're dealing with more than mere shadows or mirages after all; don't you agree? But I'm not going to let you, my dear Hans, make my merry Vienna gloomy, or you, my dear Stefan, make my living Vienna historical. Go ahead and despise me if you will. The two of you have already managed to corrupt my most sacred Viennese sensibilities. I even found myself listening to Guschelbauer the other day—that delightful ditty about the "Old Night Owl"—without feeling a thing.*

Praises are sung to the heart of gold that beats in the breast of every true Viennese, and I forget that I possess one myself! Rhymes involving "waltz" and "schmalz" leave me virtually unmoved—and I was close to mocking the notion that the tower of the good old Stefansdom or even old father Radetzky could look down on us with interest. This has all got to stop. I must regain my innocence. I want to rediscover for myself my merry, carefree Vienna, the Vienna that none of you have eyes to see. Wherever you look, Hans, all you can see is the mute melancholy of things and the blithe ignorance of people.—Max, you see yourself surrounded by arid laws and necessity.—And as for you, Stefan! Your world is full of bit players who perform for you without realizing it. Sometimes you have the goodness to applaud, but more often than not, you're not really paying attention or else you're not in the mood to listen.—I want to be different from all of you! I want to

---

* The celebrated Edmund Guschelbauer (1839–1912) wrote scores of Viennese dialect songs, performing them in the city's taverns and popular theatres.

do what none of you are actually capable of—living with them, being one of them.'

'In a word, you want to amuse yourself,' Hans said, somewhat contemptuously.

'No, I want to live among them, as one of them. I want to make my way through everything Vienna has to offer, as youth, dissolution and adventure lead me.'

'Let's hope you—of all people—are able to muster the necessary naivety,' was Max's comment.

'Me?'

'Yes, you! For you're nothing more than a covert local patriot. You feel the childish need to be fond of your fellow men, and because your mediocre heart is not big enough to love the whole world, you content yourself with the tiny speck of dust that you know best.'

'I love it—that much I will admit—but I don't know it. And I want to get to know it! What do I know, really? I know the streets, the buildings, I understand the dialect, I can see the differences between types of people and social circles, I know about promenading on the Ring, amusements in the Prater, bands playing in the courtyard of the Hofburg palace—but what gives these things their savour? Why is it that we are often pervaded by the city's soul, in all its poignant intensity, on a solitary walk in the Prater, or on the old square in front of the Minoritenkirche or at a chance word from a sweet Viennese girl, that's what I want to know!'

'Well, yes,' said Hans, 'the mystery of changing moods!'

'I was thinking about all this the other day,' Stefan remarked. 'Our ancestors' virtues and vices, their talents and prejudices don't just disappear, do they? We inherit them. Why shouldn't it be the same with moods? And when moments of enjoyment or suffering are veiled by a twilight beyond our comprehension, perhaps it's because the moods of centuries past are coursing through our souls and we simply do not recognize them as our ancestors' dreams. For we have records of their virtues and vices—but only rarely of their dreams.'

'You mystic,' said Max, 'you do nothing but confuse the matter. It's high time we trained our eyes to see the threads connecting everything. Moods only arise where there is a certain fatigue of mind and the senses. If we were always fully awake or, even better, if we were to strive for that ideal state of alertness in which all the senses are perfectly receptive, then there would be no billowing veil between us and the transparency of things, none of the shadings of mood.'

Darkness had fallen. The lanterns in the streets had been lit. The friends set off on their way back into the city.

'No, no,' said Hans. 'It's not transparency I crave! How unbearably monotonous it would make everything seem!

Life would be as frosty as a winter's day, and we would hurry through it in a fit of the sulks.'

'What do you think,' asked Max, 'which of us has the best prospects of solving the mystery that we are about to stroll back into, whose thousand streetlights and illuminated windows mock us with their gleam?—You, Hans, for whom the answer to the riddle lies in unconscious pain—or you, Stefan, for whom it seems to waft on the breeze of times gone by—or you, Fritz, with your yearning to be swept along by the unthinking throng?'

'Well, any one of us rather than you,' said Stefan, 'especially if you are really as alert as you would have us believe. But you are bound to the city as well—in a relationship that goes beyond that of spectator and spectacle. Vienna betrayed you, plain and simple, and now, like anyone who has been betrayed, you resort to coldness and mockery. Vienna was unfaithful to you because you loved it too much. You were intoxicated by it. It gave you so much: only consider—you have the city to thank for almost everything: its air inspired all that you created, your every experience was imbued with the sweetness of its atmosphere. Am I right?'

'Yes. But that's all in the past now. Vienna!—all of a sudden, the city turned its back on me. All my endeavours failed, in life and in art. I called it failure, although nothing had actually changed except for my way of seeing things.

I'm not complaining—it was bound to happen, it would have been the same anywhere else in the world. There are people who never manage to shake off their youth—like all of you, for example! But people like me wake up one morning and find that they just don't want to be part of the game any more. Then comes a period of—perhaps inevitable—bitterness, when they envy those who carry on playing. At first their only sensation is the staleness of loss. Yes, loss—they have lost the childlike joy of getting so close to things that you can touch them. They have lost their family, they don't belong any more. And for a while they are lonely and wretched, because it is not maturity that makes us lonely, but rather loneliness that matures us. But then clarity dawns. They simply allow their senses to take everything in. They stop playing games with the world, all those games to which you give so many fanciful names. I've not quite reached the point of being glad that I've given them up yet, but just wait until my senses have finally attained that "total awareness". Perhaps then I'll be able to tell you things that will amaze you. All that any of you know at the moment is whatever you yourselves have to say about life. Answers come from the depths of your soul and you think that the world has spoken.'

The friends walked on towards the city. They said nothing for a while. As they drew closer to the milling crowds where all words would be lost, Hans said:

'I'm still glad that none of the rest of us will ever attain the awareness you long for, Max.'

'But isn't it what you are looking for as well?' exclaimed Max heatedly. 'None of you is capable of peacefully enjoying your joys and sadness either. Are you really content simply to love something or to hate it? You are searching for the last great secrets too, for the soul of things.'

'Could be,' said Stefan. 'And perhaps that's why we long for things that we already have—and feel homesick when we're at home already!'

Notes on the Authors

Arthur Schnitzler (1862–1931), was born in Vienna and spent his whole life there, working first as a doctor and then as a playwright and author. He kept a detailed diary that serves scholars of *fin-de-siècle* Vienna as an invaluable index to the concerns and in-fighting of the age. Schnitzler's autobiography, *My Youth in Vienna*, gives a fascinating insight into the strains and stresses of growing up as a Jewish intellectual in an increasingly anti-Semitic society.

Joseph Roth (1894–1939), also of Jewish origin, came to Vienna in 1914 from Brody in Galicia, on the eastern rim of the Habsburg Empire. Although he spent most of his later life in Berlin and Paris, Vienna remained a focus of his writing. He portrayed the city as the quintessence of the polyglot empire that was lost forever in 1918. The reportages translated here come from the period immediately after the First World War, when 'red Roth' wrote for short-lived socialist newspapers.

Friedericke Mayröcker (b. 1924) has lived in Vienna all her life. She began publishing shortly after the Second World War but worked as an English teacher for many years before turning to writing full time in the late 1960s. Mayröcker is one of Austria's most prominent experimental poets. The free, associative style of her lyrical works also colours her prose writing and radio plays.

Alexander Kluge (b. 1932) is perhaps best known for his film and television work, in particular for his association with the New German Film movement of the 1970s. He has little to do with Vienna per se, but has been included here because of his inimitable documentary style and intense preoccupation with the mechanics of history. His description of the 1945 bombing of the Vienna Opera comes from *Chronik der Gefühle* (Chronicle of Emotions), an overwhelming 2000-page anthology, which—in ironic contrast to its title—seeks to avoid pathos by telling stories of physical cause and effect.

Anton Kuh (1890–1941), was born to a family of journalists in Vienna and died in exile, like so many other Jewish writers of his generation. He used his gift for satire to alert his contemporaries to the dangers of Vienna's polarized politics in the interwar period. Kuh was a celebrated public speaker, whose entertaining tirades would earn him the designation of stand-up comic today. The importance of the spoken word is also apparent in his journalism, which often refers to Viennese peculiarities of pronunciation and inflection.

Ingeborg Bachmann (1926–73) came to Vienna as a student from the southern Austrian province of Carinthia in the late 1940s. She first became known as a poet and author of radio plays. In 1953, Bachmann left the city to spend most of the rest of her life in Italy. Nevertheless, Vienna remained central to her fictional prose, not only to short stories such as 'O Happy Eyes', but also to longer works (see suggestions for further reading).

Heinrich Laube (1806–84), theatre critic and director, was a native of Silesia in eastern Prussia. He first visited Vienna in 1834 as part of an extended trip to Italy. The resulting travel reportages ('Reiseskizzen') were published during the late 1830s, including the piece translated here. This turbulent period saw Laube arrested in several German states due to the energy with which he defended his progressive political beliefs in the press. Following the abortive 1848 revolutions, he settled in Vienna, working first as director of the court theatre, the Burgtheater, and then of the new Stadttheater.

Ferdinand Kürnberger (1821–79) was a largely self-taught writer of short prose. Although born in Vienna and resident there for much of his life, he never ceased to goad his fellow Viennese with accounts of their complacency and parochialism. Kürnberger was forced to flee the city after participating in an uprising in October 1848, but returned in the mid-1850s. He failed to establish himself permanently at any newspaper or cultural institution, and moved to Graz during the final years of his life.

Dimitré Dinev (b. 1968) was born in Plovdiv in Bulgaria and attended a German-language grammar school. He wrote his first works in Bulgarian and Russian. In 1990, Dinev entered Austria as an illegal immigrant. Like Spas in the tale translated here, he spent time in the Traiskirchen camp and attended Vienna University on a student visa. He has since established himself as a German-language author of novels, plays, and short stories. Many of his works engage with the fates of refugees and transnational families.

Adalbert Stifter (1805–68) arrived in Vienna in 1826 to study law, an endeavour he never completed. Having grown up in modest circumstances in rural Bohemia and Upper Austria, he found life in the city difficult, but eventually found a niche as writer, landscape painter, and tutor to the offspring of Viennese high society. His prose works are now celebrated as masterpieces of the Biedermeier, in particular their immensely detailed evocations of nature. The comparatively early work translated here is one of twelve feuilletons written 1841–4 as a study of 'Vienna and the Viennese'. Stifter aimed to capture the extreme contrasts of urban life; his atmospheric descriptions also contain hints of the unrest that came to a head in 1848/9.

Veza Canetti (1897–1963) was long known only as the wife of novelist and thinker Elias Canetti. Her own writing career was cut short in 1934 by the fall of Red Vienna and never revitalized in British exile. It was not until many years after her death and shortly before her husband's that her works were republished, or in some cases, published for the first time. Canetti was of Sephardic extraction and suffered from anti-Semitic as well as political persecution before leaving Vienna. Although she took a bleak view of human nature in much of her fiction, she saw potential for solidarity and renewal in a pragmatic socialism that is often embodied in children in her works.

Christine Nöstlinger (b. 1936) is Austria's most successful children's author. She has lived in Vienna all her life. Her characters are rebellious and adventurous, like her first creation 'fire-red Friedericke', or else unworldly and naive, like 'Konrad the factory-made boy' (who comes out of a tin can). Whatever the case, they turn adult preconceptions upside down. Although Nöstlinger's figures often manage to break out of everyday routine, her stories are not escapist; she does not shy away from serious or potentially disturbing topics. Her postwar childhood in the working-class district of Hernals inspired the piece included here.

Eva Menasse (b. 1970), was born in Vienna and studied literature and history at Vienna University. She began her career as a journalist, and became an editor of Germany's most prominent daily, the *Frankfurter Allgemeine Zeitung*. Her first book was a collection of reports on the London trial of holocaust denier David Irving. Menasse now lives in Berlin as an author of short stories and novels (see suggestions for further reading). Her often strongly autobiographical works tell Vienna's history by probing the cracks in its modern-day veneer.

Doron Rabinovici (b. 1961), a native of Tel Aviv, moved to Vienna as a child in 1964. The tale translated here comes from his first collection of short stories *Papirnik* (1995), which revolves around the dilemmas of Austrian-Israeli and Austrian-Jewish identity. Other stories available in English include 'The Right Nose' (translated by Dagmar C. Lorenz in *Nothing Makes You Free*, 2003). As well as publishing fiction, Rabinovici is a historian and political activist. *Eichmann's Jews*, a study of the ways in which Vienna's Jewish community was forced to collude with the National Socialist regime, came out in English in 2011.

Further Reading

Guide Books

The Lonely Planet and Time Out guides to Vienna are good, as is the 2012 National Geographic traveller guide with its beautiful images. The Blue Guide to Vienna, although last published in 2002, is still well worth perusing for its cultural and historical detail. Those arriving by air can quickly find out what's on in the city from the garish but free English-language magazine pushed into their hands just before baggage reclaim. Otherwise, the best place to look for detailed, up-to-date information is the twice monthly *Der Falter* (event, restaurant, and club listings as well as political commentary). *Der Falter* also publishes the best book-length guide to Vienna's eateries, *Wien, wie es isst*, updated annually. Look out in particular for its recommendations of 'Heurige', the rustic wine bars mostly situated in out-of-the-way locations around the city's edge. They are only open for brief windows of a month or so at a time—precise advance information is crucial.

Fans of public transport will enjoy the wonderful historical photographs in Elfriede Faber and Heinz Jankowsky, *Linien, die verbinden: Mit Straßenbahn und Bus durch Wien* (Sutton Verlag, 2008), a guide book through the ages that criss-crosses the city along its tram and bus lines. The recently revitalized Gürtel area can be explored using a richly illustrated volume put together by Green Party politician Madeleine Petrovic, *Der Wiener Gürtel* (Brandstätter, 2009). Good guides to footpaths in the Vienna Woods include the paperback Rother Walking Guide *Vienna—Vienna Woods* (2013). Keen hikers should also consult the Rother Walking Guide to the 'Wiener Hausberge', Vienna's 'house mountains', as the nearest of the Alpine peaks are known.

History and Reference Books about Vienna

Fin-de-Siècle Vienna. Politics and Culture by Carl E. Schorske (Knopf, 1980, republished many times since). Pulitzer-prize-winning account of the city's architecture, design, literature, and music in the glory days around 1900, complete with sumptuous black and white illustrations. Schorske is credited with ushering in a whole new era of interdisciplinary scholarship on Vienna, and revolutionizing the way the Viennese see the history of their own city.

Vienna and the Jews. A Cultural History 1867–1938 by Steven Beller (Cambridge University Press, 1991), a persuasive attempt to explain why Jewish figures were so prevalent among Vienna's cultural and intellectual elite from the late nineteenth century to the advent of Nazism.

Vienna and the Fall of the Habsburg Empire by Maureen Healy (Cambridge University Press, 2004), as the subtitle says, a study of 'total war and everyday life in World War I'.

The Siege of Vienna by John Stoye (Collins 1964, revised and republished by Pegasus, 2000), a gripping account of the final Ottoman siege of Vienna in 1683 that includes background information on the development of Habsburg Vienna over the sixteenth and seventeenth centuries. The maps provided help understand how the city's present topography came about.

The Architecture of Red Vienna by Eve Blau (MIT Press, 1999) gives an excellent introduction to the culture and politics of the years of the interwar Social Democrat administration 1918–34. A handsome volume with lots of photographs.

Political Radicalism in Late Imperial Vienna (University of Chicago Press, 1981) and *Culture and Political Crisis in Vienna* (University of Chicago Press, 1995) by John Boyer. Two volumes of impressive depth and detail charting the development of the Viennese middle class 1848–1918, with an emphasis on populist politics and the rise of anti-Semitism as a political tool.

Hitler's Vienna: A Dictator's Apprenticeship (Oxford University Press, 1999, paperback 2010 Tauris/Palgrave Macmillan) by Brigitte Harmann, combines social and cultural history with an account of Hitler's coming of age. *Fin-de-siècle* Vienna is seen here from the perspective of the struggling would-be artist from the provinces with a huge chip on his shoulder.

Vienna: A Cultural History by Nicolas Parsons (Oxford University Press, 2009). By the same author as the informative Blue Guide on Vienna, this eminently readable volume functions as both guide book and reference history. Parsons simultaneously revels in and deconstructs clichés of the city; the personal slant in no way detracts from the thorough research behind the factual content.

Tante Hertha's Viennese Kitchen. A Book of Family Recipes by Monica Meehan and Maria von Baich (New Holland Publishers, 2011). Readers gain insight, not only into Viennese cuisine, but also into the city's history as seen through the eyes of a family who seem to have been largely unaffected by the caesurae of 1938 and 1945. The many photographs of the city make it look as appetizing as the dishes described, but are devoid of captions. A book for confirmed Vienna fans rather than first-timers.

The Viennese Café and Fin-de-Siècle Culture, edited by Charlotte Ashby, Tag Gronberg, and Simon Shaw-Miller (Berghahn, 2013). A refreshingly multi-perspectival look at one of Vienna's most popular institutions. Although aimed at an academic rather than general readership, this study—as one would hope, given its subject matter—is nevertheless full of gossip and anecdotes.

German Short Stories and Prose about Vienna

Dream Story by Arthur Schnitzler, authorized translation by J. M. Q. Davies in 1926, reissued by Penguin Classics in 1999 with an informative introduction by Frederic Raphael. This miniature psychological thriller is grounded by the topographical precision of its Viennese setting.

The Thirtieth Year by Ingeborg Bachmann, translated by Michael Bullock (Andre Deutsch 1964, republished by Polygon in 1993). Of these seven experimental, often disturbing tales, all but one are set in Vienna and seek to explain the attraction and repulsion of the city and its history.

Prose by Thomas Bernhard, translated by Martin Chalmers (Seagull, 2010). 'Is it a Comedy? Is it a Tragedy?' has a lot to say about Vienna's traditions of theatricality and the macabre, and 'The Crime of an Innsbruck Shopkeeper's Son' comments on the relationship between capital and provinces.

'The Poor Fiddler' or 'The Poor Musician' by Franz Grill-parzer (1847) is available in various translations, of which the most fluent is by Richard Hacken (in *Into the Sunset: Anthology of Nineteenth-Century Austrian Prose*, Ariadne Press, 1999, also available in a Kindle edition). The inef-fectual and yet immensely appealing Jakob, failed son, lover, and musician, sacrifices himself for others and for his art, bringing together the margins and centre of Viennese society. This gem of a novella is an exception in the oeuvre of an author best-known as a dramatist and poet.

Vienna Spring. Early Novellas and Stories by Stefan Zweig, translated by William Ruleman (Ariadne Press, 2010). Touching variations on the theme of youth and its uncer-tainties, written as Zweig was growing up in Vienna. Readers should not be tempted to read the translator's afterword before the stories themselves—although informative and empathetic, it's full of spoilers!

Veza Canetti, *Viennese Short Stories*, translated by Julian Preece (Ariadne Press, 2006). Canetti's unique brand of socialist realism, rediscovered long after her death.

German Novels about Vienna

Malina, by Ingeborg Bachmann, translated by Philip Boehm (Holmes and Meier, 1999). A feminist classic. The tormented protagonist seeks refuge in Vienna's third district, only to discover that nowhere is safe...

Yellow Street, by Veza Canetti, translated by Ian Mitchell (New Directions, 1991). Scurrilous episodes in the life of a predominantly Jewish area of the city during the interwar period.

The Demons by Heimito von Doderer, translated by Richard and Clara Winston (Alfred A. Knopf, 1961). Fiction dovetails with historical fact in this immensely detailed chronicle of a Viennese clique in the years 1926–7.

Wittgenstein's Nephew by Thomas Bernhard, translated by David McLintock (first published by Knopf, 1988, republished by Faber, 2013). A slim autobiographical novel about the author's friendship with Paul Wittgenstein. Typical Bernhardian tirades against Viennese cafés, Viennese writers, Viennese civil servants and Viennese theatre life are juxtaposed with grudging recognition for the city's musical and intellectual heritage.

The Piano Teacher by Elfriede Jelinek, translated by Joachim Neugroschel (Serpent's Tail, 2010). Vienna, city of music? A grotesque yet compelling deconstruction. See also the 2001 film adaptation by Michael Haneke.

The Man without Qualities by Robert Musil, translated by Sophie Wilkins and Burton Pike. Musil's vast unfinished work is set in Vienna just before the outbreak of the First World War.

The Road into the Open by Arthur Schnitzler, translated by Roger Byers (University of California Press, 1992, also available in the first authorized English translation by Horace Samuel published in 1913, available online via Cornell University Library). Talented yet lacking in drive, the composer Georg Wergenthin is a Christian aristocrat who socializes largely with upper-middle-class Jews against the backdrop of rising anti-Semitism. The elegance and naturalness of Schnitzler's prose is perhaps best rendered by the more recent of the two translations.

Vienna Passion by Lilian Faschinger, translated by Anthea Bell (Headline, 2000). Biting satire on contemporary Vienna, seen through the bewildered eyes of a young New Yorker with Viennese roots.

Eva Menasse, *Vienna* translated by Anthea Bell (Phoenix, 2007), another tour de force from one of German-language literature's most prolific and talented English translators. This retrospective family saga brings Jewish Vienna up-to-date in a highly entertaining yet thought-provoking manner.

Arno Geiger, *We are doing fine,* translated by Maria Poglitsch Bauer (Ariadne Press, 2011). A dilapidated villa and three generations of an increasingly uncommunicative family tell the tale of Vienna's twentieth-century history.

Memoirs about Vienna

My Youth in Vienna by Arthur Schnitzler, translated by Catherine Hutter (Weidenfeld & Nicolson, 1971) with a foreword by A. J. P. Taylor. Confessions of a philanderer combined with first-hand insights into the (self-)contradictions of the city's *fin-de-siècle.*

The World of Yesterday by Stefan Zweig, translated by Anthea Bell (Pushkin Press, 2009). First published posthumously in exile, this nostalgic look at the final years of Habsburg Vienna nevertheless gives a clear-sighted appraisal of the clientelism and sexual hypocrisy of the times.

The Tongue Set Free, The Torch in My Ear, The Play of the Eyes by Elias Canetti, translated by Joachim Neugroschel (Granta, 2011). Three-volume account of the author's youth spent largely in interwar Vienna. Highly subjective yet informative in many ways and very readable.

Publisher's Acknowledgements

1) Arthur Schnitzler, 'The Four-poster Bed' from *Entworfenes und Verworfenes. Aus dem Nachlass* (*Gesammelte Werke*, volume 6), edited by Reinhard Urbach, S. Fischer Verlag, 1977, pp. 72–77.

2) Joseph Roth, 'Day Out' from *Das journalistische Werk 1915–1923* (*Werke*, volume 1) edited by Klaus Westermann, Kiepenheuer & Witsch, 1989, pp. 269–271.

3) Friedericke Mayröcker, 'Vienna 1924 to', from *Magische Blätter V*
© Suhrkamp Verlag, 1999

4) Alexander Kluge, 'The Twilight of the Gods in Vienna' from *Chronik der Gefühle*
© Suhrkamp Verlag, 2000

5) Anton Kuh, 'Lenin and Dehmel' from *Luftlinien. Feuilletons, Essays und Publizistik*, edited by Ruth Greuner, Löcker Verlag, 1981, pp. 92–94.

6) Ingeborg Bachmann, 'Ihr glücklichen Augen', from
Werke 2. Erzählungen.
© Piper Verlag GmbH, Munich, 1978

7) Heinrich Laube, 'Vienna' *from Der Theatercaesar,*
Stiasny Verlag, 1958, pp. 58–61.

8) Ferdinand Kürnberger, 'The Feuilletonists' from
Klassiker des Feuilletons, edited by Hans Bender,
Reclam 1965, pp. 44–57.

9) Dimitré Dinev, 'Spas schläft', from *Ein Licht über
dem Kopf.*
© Deuticke im Paul Zsolnay Verlag, Wien, 2005

10) Joseph Roth, 'The Spring Ship' from *Das
journalistische Werk 1915–1923* (*Werke*, volume 1)
edited by Klaus Westermann, Kiepenheuer & Witsch,
1989, pp. 279–281.

11) Adalbert Stifter, 'The Prater' from *Wien und die
Wiener in Bildern aus dem Leben (1844)*, edited by
Elisabeth Buxbaum, LIT Verlag, 2005, pp. 208–218.

12) Veza Canetti, 'Der Verbrecher' from *Geduld bringt
Rosen.*
© Canetti Erben, Zürich, 1992
© Carl Hanser Verlag, München, 1992

13) Christine Nöstlinger, 'Ottakringerstraße' from
Tintenfisch. Jahrbuch für Literatur (volume 13, 1978),
pp. 110–114.

14) Eva Menasse, *Neid*.
© Verlag Kiepenheuer & Witsch GmbH & Co, KG, Vienna/Köln, 2005.

15) Doron Rabinovici, '696969', from *Papirnik*.
© Suhrkamp Verlag, 1994

16) Joseph Roth, 'Merry-go-round' from *Das journalistische Werk 1915–1923* (*Werke*, volume 1) edited by Klaus Westermann, Kiepenheuer & Witsch, 1989, pp. 266–267.

17) Arthur Schnitzler, 'Out for a Walk' from *Entworfenes und Verworfenes. Aus dem Nachlass* (*Gesammelte Werke*, volume 6), edited by Reinhard Urbach, S. Fischer Verlag, 1977, pp. 152–156.

References.

1. The Castle
2. City Hospital
3. Chranen
4. The Mint
5. Salt Store House
6. The Arsenal
7. The Foundery
8. St Peter
9. St George
10. Augustins Convent
11. The Pauliner
12. Little Father Convent
13. St Catherine
14. Cordeliers Convent
15. Hall Sant
16. Capuchin Convent
17. St Agnes
18. St John
19. St Ursulle
20. St James
21. St Ignace
22. Jacobins Convent
23. Benedictins Convent
24. St Elizabeth
25. Magdalen Church
26. The Hall
27. Our Lady
28. Carmelites
29. Town Hall
30. St Leopold
31. Nusdorff Gate
32. The Hospital
33. Lerchenfeld Gate
34. Mariahalf Gate
35. Royal Mill
36. St Egidi
37. Jesuits Convent
38. Dominician Convent
39. Starenberg
40. Neuerberg Gate
41. Favourite Gate
42. St Mark
43. St Mark's Gate
44. St Roch
45. The Jesuits

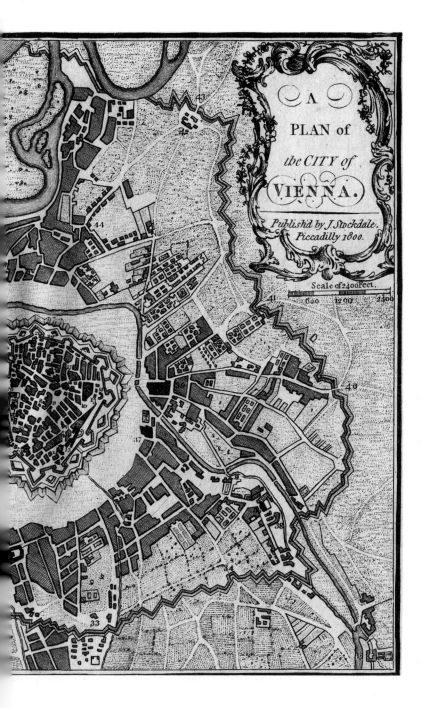

A

PLAN of

the CITY of

VIENNA.

Publish'd by J.Stockdale.
Piccadilly 1800.

Scale of 2400 Feet.

600   1200   2400